Praise for Tish Westwood's
Scarlet Kisses

"This clever book is a great read. The characters sparkle with wit and charm, and the hero and heroine's complex relationship is a delight to watch play out. The dialogue, especially when the characters start to bicker, is very fun. Fans of erotica will be blown away by the story's off-the-charts sexual tension."

~ *RT Book Reviews*

"This is a truly charming novel that I had a very difficult time putting down. I thoroughly enjoyed the characters, their attitudes, their development, and the story itself. I am wholeheartedly looking forward to the rest of the series... Romantics everywhere will love this. I certainly did."

~ *Night Owl Reviews*

Look for these titles by *Tish Westwood*

Now Available:

Passions Unveiled

Scarlet Kisses

Scarlet Kisses

Tish Westwood

SAMHAIN
PUBLISHING

Samhain Publishing, Ltd.
11821 Mason Montgomery Road, 4B
Cincinnati, OH 45249
www.samhainpublishing.com

Editing by Heidi Moore
Cover by Lyn Taylor

First Samhain Publishing, Ltd. electronic publication: June 2012
First Samhain Publishing, Ltd. print publication: May 2013

Dedication

To my amazing family, Mum, Dad, Nick, Sam and AJ. You guys are unreal.

Chapter One

Year 1843

"You are a good, respectable and proper woman," Travis Potting said as he sat before Alyssum in the front parlor of her family's country estate. His hands were folded tightly in his lap and his brow sweat in nervousness. "That is why it is difficult for me to tell you..." He squeezed his hands tighter. "I will be unable to go forth with this courtship."

Alyssum sat quietly on her chair as she listened to Mr. Potting's announcement. Her hands that had been lying in her lap were now clutched together. This was not happening. Travis was supposed to marry her. They were supposed to live a quiet, simple life in his vicarage. That was how she had wanted it. That was what she had planned. Quiet and simple. Now it was all ruined.

"May I ask why?" she asked, her polite smile still frozen on her lips.

"I have fallen in love with another," he announced with a rise of his pointed chin.

"Who?" she asked before she could stop herself.

Travis shifted in his seat uncomfortably. "Miss Clarice Weathers."

"Miss Weathers?" Alyssum repeated breathlessly. She could picture her now. Long, curling blonde hair, baby-blue eyes, voluptuous figure and big bouncing breasts. At eighteen and just revealed by low-cut gowns, she was the toast of the county and men now flocked to her. They reminded her of a coop of chickens pecking, and Clarice was the bucket of feed.

While Alyssum usually stood with her sister or her mother, Miss Clarice Weathers was always found jumping around on the dance floor and twittering like a bird.

"I had no idea. Does Miss Weathers feel the same way about you?" she asked.

"Well...yes. I mean...we haven't spoken of our feelings...yet. But I believe she does, yes," he stuttered out.

"Then I wish you both all the happiness in the world." Alyssum managed a brighter smile.

"I'm so glad you understand," Travis sighed, his relief obvious. "Well, I must be leaving." He stood and Alyssum followed suit. They bowed and curtseyed to one another.

"I'll let myself out."

"Good day, Mr. Potting."

"And to you." He nodded before leaving the parlor.

Alyssum stared after him, watching the empty doorway. She sighed deeply. Now who was she going to marry? At twenty-two she was beginning to worry she would become a spinster. She didn't want to be a lonely, old spinster. She wanted a husband and a house and children. How would she ever get them if nobody would marry her? Travis Potting was a sweet man, a man of God. He would have made her a suitable husband and given her the things she craved. She may not love him, but they would have been content together.

"Meg?" Alyssum looked over to the young maid sitting in the corner quietly.

"Yes, miss?"

"Please don't speak of this until I have spoken to my mother."

"Yes, miss." She nodded.

Alyssum walked from the room. Entering the foyer, she saw a man standing with his back to her. Her heart hit the wall of her chest and her belly fluttered. She exhaled, annoyed with her reaction to this man.

"Viscount Lambert," Alyssum greeted him with a blasé attitude.

Turning quickly when his name was called, Robert looked to Alyssum and gave her a bright smile that had broken so many debutant hearts. With disheveled brown hair, a constant gleam of mischief in his brown eyes and an askew cravat, he was judged to be one of the most reckless and daring man of the ton.

"Alyssum." He gave her an exaggerated bow. With one arm out to the side, he gave her a sweeping bow then swung back straight. She returned his bow with a small, quick curtsy.

"As always, a pleasure to see you," he said as he continued smiling at her, but now the smile had turned more into a grin in her judgment. Did the man ever not have that wicked glint in his eyes?

The untidiness of his cravat grated her teeth. After a quick glance to make sure there were no servants about, she stormed over to him. His grin flashed brighter as she approached. He chuckled as she grabbed his coats lapels and made him bend down to her. She unraveled his cravat then retied it quickly and efficiently. She stepped back and surveyed the straight cravat with approval.

"Couldn't keep your hands off me, could you?" he murmured.

She met his gaze and jerked backwards when she found them standing so close. She could see the gold flakes in his brown eyes. She took another step back, placing the proper distance between them.

"Are you waiting for Harry?" she asked, changing the topic hurriedly as she noticed the folder in his hand.

"Yes," he replied. "And how many times must I tell you to call me Robert?" He took a step forward, breaking the appropriate distance between them.

"It would not be proper," she replied, and took a step back.

"But we've known each other since we were kids. I live next door. We used to throw mud at each other."

Alyssum shifted her gaze around the empty foyer.

"Ah, wouldn't want someone to hear you used to have fun," he whispered.

"I still have fun," she snapped and turned her gaze back to his.

"Really? What was the last fun thing you did?" He folded his arms over his chest and waited for her answer.

"Well..." she trailed off with a slight frown. She couldn't think of anything off the top of her head.

"And so help me God, if you say embroidering..." He closed his eyes and looked as if he were in pain.

"It can be fun," she snapped.

Robert chuckled and shook his head. "Tsk, tsk. What am I going to do with you, Alyssum?"

"You're not going to do anything with my sister," a firm voice broke in.

Robert and Alyssum turned their gazes over to Harry, who stood before his open study door.

"Please?" Robert beseeched, his eyes playful.

Harry glared at him then looked over to Alyssum. "Is Mr. Potting gone?"

"Mr. Potting?" Robert looked back to Alyssum. "Really?" He

arched a brow incredulously.

Ignoring Robert, Alyssum kept her gaze on Harry. "Yes, he left," she told her brother.

"He didn't..." Harry looked at her expectantly.

"No, and he will not."

Harry gave her sympathetic look.

"You wanted to marry Travis Potting, the vicar?" Robert cried out with a look of horror on his face.

Alyssum looked back to him with irritation. "Good day, Viscount Lambert," she snipped out.

His grin came back and he gave her another exaggerated bow. "Alyssum."

"It's Lady Rosewood to you," Harry said.

"I don't call women I've swum naked with by their titles," Robert informed them.

Harry groaned while Alyssum made a noise of outrage.

"I have never," she exclaimed with her cheeks flushed red.

"You have." Robert smiled wickedly.

"I was young, and I always wore my shift."

"The shift was white and you were wet. I've seen you naked," he whispered the last bit.

Harry stalked over to Robert, grabbed him by the collar of his shirt, yanked him away from Alyssum and pulled him into his office.

Shutting his office door with a loud bang, Harry then shoved Robert further into the room.

"Why?" Harry asked as he sat down behind his desk. "Why do you have to torment my sister?"

"It's so much fun." Robert dropped the folder onto the table then sat and perched his feet onto Harry's desk. "I love making the prim and proper squirm and blush." He grinned like the devil he was.

"That fact wouldn't have anything to do with why the Earl of Blackmore glares at you every time he sees you, would it?" He pushed Robert's feet off his desk.

"Yes, it does," Robert announced proudly. "I told his daughter how the French kiss."

"Told not taught?" Harry arched brow.

"She's a debutant," Robert said, as if that explained everything. Which it did. Robert would never mix with a debutant unless he wanted to get married, which he didn't. Not for at least another ten years, and only because he needed an heir. He was only twenty-eight. He had plenty of time until he had to chain himself down.

"All right, down to business." Harry leaned forward and opened the folder Robert had brought.

"All right." Robert sighed and also leaned forward. He always came to Harry, his best friend since childhood, for business matters. He knew his endless supply of family fortune was still rising with the help of Harry. Without Harry sitting on his shoulder, being his guardian angel, he would have gambled and whored it all away when his old man died ten years ago. When that joyous occasion had finally come, Robert had burned his father's office to a crisp, with the help of a certain person. Luckily, the servants were quick or they may have accidentally burned the whole house down.

"That man!" Alyssum huffed in anger as she paced the carpeted floor of her sister's room.

"You shouldn't let him get to you this way," Violet said from the window seat, a book in her lap.

"I have fun," Alyssum snapped and turned to Violet. "Right?" she asked, unsure.

"Of course you have fun."

"Yes. You're right, I do have fun. I am a fun person." She began pacing again.

Violet gave a small shake of her head and turned her attention back to the book of poetry on her lap.

"I can't think of anything." Alyssum stopped pacing and faced Violet again.

"Pardon?"

"I can't think of anything fun I've done lately."

"What about your gardening?" Violet volunteered.

Alyssum tilted her head to the side. "I guess I enjoy it. But I wouldn't say it's fun."

"Well, who cares what Robert thinks?"

"Robert?" Alyssum raised her eyebrows to Violet.

Violet shifted in her seat. "Well, we did grow up together. I've known him all my life."

"But it's not proper."

Violet rolled her eyes.

"Violet Rosewood." Alyssum placed her hands on her slender hips. "Did you just roll your eyes at me?"

Violet opened her mouth to protest when Jasmine, the youngest Rosewood sibling, ran into the room and slammed the door shut behind her. Panting for breath with her long black hair falling about her shoulders wildly, she gasped, "Help me. Hide me from Mother."

"What have you done now, Jaz?" Violet asked.

"Nothing." She tried looking innocent.

"Jasmine Rosewood," Alyssum spoke with authority.

"Yes, Alyssum Rosewood," Jaz mocked her and hopped onto the bed with a bounce.

Violet hid her smile behind her book.

"What are we all doing?" Jaz asked.

"Discussing the last fun thing we did," Violet answered.

"Oh, joy." A knock came at the door and Jaz jumped from the bed in a flash.

"Yes?" Violet called.

"Violet, dear, is Jasmine in there?" Their mother's voice was muffled through the door.

"Yes, she is," Violet called back.

"Traitor," Jaz whispered.

The door swung open to reveal their mother. "Jasmine," Caroline said disapprovingly with her gaze on her youngest.

"It wasn't me," Jaz was quick to exclaim.

"So you didn't use a servant's mattress to slide down the servants' stairs?" their mother placed her hands on her hips. Her black hair and green eyes were identical to Jaz and Alyssum's. Even at fifty, she still possessed the same beauty that had captured their father's heart.

"Perhaps," Jaz drawled.

"Your room, now." Caroline pointed down the hall.

Grudgingly complying with her mother's order, Jasmine strode from the room, dragging her feet all the way.

"I'm terrified of the day we introduce her into society," Caroline spoke quietly.

"Society already knows Jasmine," Alyssum said.

"Not in the ballrooms," replied their mother.

"Try not to worry," Violet replied in her soothing voice.

"She's only sixteen. She'll settle down."

"Perhaps in Paris?" their mother asked.

Violet twisted her lips while Alyssum replied, "It would do her some good. Paris worked for me."

"Yes, it did." Their mother smiled brightly. "I don't think I would have survived another one of your pranks. I'll talk to Jasmine." There was a pause before she asked Alyssum, "How is Mr. Potting?"

"In love," Alyssum replied and then watched as her mother's face lit up. "With Clarice Weathers," she finished and watched her mother's smile drop.

"I'm so sorry, dear." The countess walked forward and touched Alyssum's arm gently. "I know how much you wanted to marry him."

Alyssum forced a smile. "I'll find another."

With a smile to both her daughters, the countess left the room.

"I'm sorry, Liss," Violet said gently.

Alyssum let her disappointment show as she dropped onto the window seat beside Violet.

"Now you'll have to go to London with the rest of us and go through another season," Violet said.

With a groan, Alyssum slouched into the cushioned seat in a very unladylike manner. She was tired. Tired of London, tired of society, tired of searching for a husband. Tired of her boring life

"Robert's right," she whispered.

Violet's eyes widened slightly at hearing Alyssum call Viscount Lambert by his first name.

Alyssum shook her head. "I don't have fun."

"Well, then go have fun," Violet urged.

"How?"

"If you want advice on fun, I know the perfect person to ask." Violet arched a brow.

Alyssum smiled, knowing who just that person was.

"What do you think?" Violet asked Jaz as they stood in her bedroom.

"Well, I think a lot of things, but right now I'm wondering how you unlocked my door?" she asked with a curious expression as she sat on the edge of her bed. She had been trying to pick the lock for three minutes with not an ounce of success. Her mother currently held the key in her pocket.

"I picked the lock," Violet replied.

"How?" Jaz asked and leaned forward in her attempt to hear the secret.

"I'll teach you how to pick the lock if you give us your opinion on the matter at hand."

"Right, right," she muttered and leaned back. "Alyssum?"

"Yes?" Alyssum replied cautiously as she stood beside Violet.

"You are salvable."

"I'm glad."

"What kind of fun are you looking for?" Jaz linked her fingers and leaned her chin on them.

Alyssum shook her head, not knowing.

"Do you want to have fun in the country or in London?"

"Both would be nice," Alyssum replied. "I want to be like I used to be," she said sadly, remembering her mischievous days.

She had been just like Jaz. Well, not quite like Jaz. Jaz was a whole new level of naughty for an innocent.

"Well, I can fix that," Jaz announced.

"Really? How?" Alyssum arched a brow.

"I will tell you, only if you do one thing for me."

"What is it?"

"Convince Mother not to send me to that school in Paris," she pleaded.

"Jaz, you were caught kissing the footman last week," Violet said as she strode over to a chair by the wall and sat down.

"And?" Jaz raised her brows.

Violet shook her head disapprovingly. "That man now has no job because of you."

Jaz turned her gaze to Alyssum with a look that said she didn't understand the problem.

Alyssum shook her head and waved her hand. "I'll talk to Mother, but I can't guarantee anything."

"Fair enough." Jaz relaxed back on her bed. "I know something fun you can do in London." She arched her brow as if daring Alyssum to ask.

"What is it?" Alyssum asked cautiously.

"Are you prepared to be naughty?" Jaz asked with that smile that usually got her locked in her room.

Alyssum looked to Violet for advice. Violet shrugged.

"Let's hear it," Alyssum answered. "How bad can it be?"

"That's it." Harry leaned back in his chair. They had finally finished going through all of Robert's papers.

Robert sighed and also leaned back in his chair. "Are you coming to London?" he asked.

Harry groaned. "I don't want to, but I have to."

"Why?" Robert demanded. He hated that his best friend tortured himself for his family. Society was vain and shallow, and because of a thin white scar marking his face from a childhood fall, Harry had been called ugly on more than one occasion.

"I have two sisters in society who need my watching," Harry answered.

"Violet and Alyssum, what trouble could they get into? They're the most sensible ladies I know."

"Compared to the other *ladies* you know, my sisters are saints," Harry replied dryly.

"Yes, they are."

"Are you still with that woman?" Harry asked Robert out of curiosity.

"Which one?"

Harry rolled his eyes and tried not to laugh. "The actress with red hair."

"*Oh,*" Robert sighed, remembering faintly. "No," he shook his head. "She got clingy. Eck." He leaned forward and crossed his arms on Harry's desk.

"Do you remember her name?" Harry asked for a laugh. He smiled as he watched Robert try to remember the woman's name. Robert wore a frown as his eyes moved back and forth as if looking through an invisible filling cabinet. Eventually the frown smoothed away and he smiled.

"You remember?" Harry said.

"No." Robert grinned.

Harry laughed and shook his head.

"Why can't your mother watch the girls?"

"Why don't you want me to go to London?" Harry asked.

"I know you hate it."

"I don't hate London." Harry sighed. "I just hate playing nice with the annoying."

"Then stay here." Robert waved his hands around the spacious study. The study that had once belonged to Harry's loving father. He watched as Harry debated with himself whether or not to go to London.

"I have to watch the girls," he finally announced.

"Do what?" Robert demanded. "Alyssum's quiet as a mouse and stays with the American girl, who, by the way, has one of the strictest chaperons in the country, while Violet sneaks off to the hostess's library and reads their books."

Harry chuckled, knowing everything Robert said about his sisters was true. "I have responsibilities."

"Fine," Robert sighed with a shake of his head.

"Stay here," Robert said. "If it helps, I'll keep an occasional eye on the girls."

"No, it doesn't help."

"I can be sensible," Robert said, then muttered under his breath, "Sometimes."

"I'll talk to Mother." Harry sighed.

"You do that."

Violet gasped, Jaz grinned and Alyssum remained silent.

"No," Violet said as she stood from her seat and walked to Alyssum.

"It'll be fun," Jaz cajoled. "And harmless."

"Harmless," Violet spoke in outrage. "She could be ruined if things go wrong."

"Why would things go wrong?" Jaz asked, and Violet began listing.

Alyssum remained quiet, thinking things over. "It sounds fun," she eventually said to break Violet's rant.

"What?" Violet spun around and looked at Alyssum with wide eyes. "You understand the plan, right?"

"Yes."

"And you're still going to do it?" she almost screamed.

"Shhh," Jaz shushed her quickly, not wanting her mother to hear.

"I'll be wearing a mask," Alyssum said.

"Oh, well, then everything will be fine," she spoke sarcastically.

"I want to do this," Alyssum said. Her gaze drifted to Jaz and her excitement rose.

"Liss, you could be caught."

"I won't be."

"What if the man that you kiss recognizes you and tells society? Is it really worth risking your whole future?"

Alyssum remained silent before replying sternly, "He won't recognize me. Besides who would believe it? Lady Alyssum Rosewood being found in a compromising position with a gentleman?" She arched a brow. "I don't think so."

Jaz clapped her hands excitedly. "Oh, I wish I could come to London."

"Soon," Violet said. Their brother and mother had both agreed to wait till Jasmine was eighteen until having her come out.

"Two years," Jaz sighed dreamily.

"I propose a test," Alyssum said to them. "I will prove that if a rumor spreads people will not believe it."

"They wouldn't dare gossip about the Earl of Leighton's sister," said Violet.

"It's strange when you call Harry by his title," Jaz laughed.

"What is this test?" Violet asked.

"I'll show you." Alyssum turned and walked from the room.

Violet strode after her while Jaz hovered in the doorway looking for any signs of her mother. Hesitating only for a moment, she then ran from her room into freedom and followed her sisters downstairs.

As Alyssum stepped off the last stair, she turned and walked over to Harry's study.

Knocking lightly on the door, she waited until Harry bid her enter.

"Enter," he called.

Alyssum took one glance at her sisters then opened the door, walked in and shut it behind her.

When the door closed softly, Alyssum knew her sisters would be pressing their ears to the wood.

"Alyssum," Harry greeted her as he and Robert stood from their chairs.

"I have something I need to tell you," she said in a serious tone.

"All right," he replied then looked to Robert. "Do you mind?"

"No," Alyssum cut in. "I would like him to hear this."

Robert frowned then, looking to Harry, he shrugged and

dropped back into his chair. He watched Harry and Alyssum as he slouched.

"What is it you wanted to say?" Harry asked, still standing.

Alyssum took a deep breath then exhaled. "When Mr. Potting was here earlier...I kissed him."

Harry stared at her in silence. And Robert... He burst into laughter. At Harry's murderous glare, he covered it by coughing and thumping his chest with his fist.

"Alyssum." Harry sighed. "I know you want to get married, but trapping a man with a lie is *not* the right thing."

Even though she had gotten the results she was looking for, she blushed brightly in embarrassment. "I'm sorry," she apologized. "It won't happen again." She turned quickly and left the room.

Standing outside Harry's study, Alyssum turned her head to the side and looked at her sisters. They both stood with wide, excited eyes.

"Well?" she whispered.

"The plan will work," Violet announced, shocked.

"Of course it will." Jaz bounced on her feet, hardly containing her excitement.

Alyssum beamed. She could hardly wait.

"Mother," Harry greeted his mother from the doorway of the countess' pink private parlor.

"Harry." She smiled happily. "Come in."

Walking into the room filled with pink, Harry tried not to cringe as he sat on the light pink settee.

"I wish to speak to you about this year's season."

"Go ahead, sweetheart."

Even at twenty-eight, Harry couldn't help but blush at the endearment. Clearing his throat, he looked at his mother. "Will you be able to chaperon the girls?"

"Of course," she replied cheerfully.

"While I stay here?" he finished.

"Oh." She seemed surprised. "You don't want to join in on the season?"

Harry wrinkled his nose. Caroline smiled and leaned over to pat his scarred cheek affectionately. "I can handle Violet and Alyssum. The girls are well behaved. Jasmine on the other hand…"

Harry winced and shook his head. "We really need to do something about her."

"I know, dear. I was thinking the school in Paris?"

Harry raised his eyebrows. "It worked for Alyssum."

"Alyssum wasn't this kind of naughty. She threw mud pies at the house and put that fish in your bed, but Jaz…" Caroline trailed off with a sigh.

"Jaz took Father's death badly," Harry said quietly. He watched as his mother took a small sip from her teacup. Her hand shook as she placed it back on the saucer. Reaching out, Harry placed his hand over hers. The loss of the late earl had hurt them all. It still hurt, but it had broken his mother's heart.

"Father died four years ago. We all grieved, but she's…" Harry shook his head. Nobody knew what ran through Jasmine's head.

"The school in Paris will do her good."

"I agree." He squeezed her hand.

"I will write to them."

Harry nodded then released her hand and settled back in his seat.

"How is Robert? Still up to no good?" Caroline asked.

"He's the same." Harry nodded with a smile. He leaned in and took a small, square sandwich off the plate that sat on the table between them.

"Will he be joining us for dinner?"

Harry nodded as he swallowed his bite of the sandwich. "Last dinner before he heads for London."

"We will be leaving the day after," she informed him. "You will take good care of Jaz."

"I will."

"Watch her. Closely."

Harry smiled at her severe tone. "I will," he promised.

Chapter Two

"Come along, girls." The countess waved as she walked ahead of them on the bustling London streets. "We have a lot to acquire before the season begins."

"Are you still going to do it?" Violet whispered to Alyssum as they walked behind their mother.

"Yes."

Violet sighed. "You can't be serious, Alyssum."

Alyssum ignored her and continued following their mother.

"Liss." Violet grabbed her by the arm with her gloved hand and pulled her to a stop. "You can't do this. It's madness."

"I want to. I'm going to," Alyssum replied firmly, her head lowered, bonnet shielding her face from onlookers. "I need your help, Vi," she whispered desperately.

Violet grumbled then let Alyssum's arm go. "All right. But if you get caught, I had nothing to do with this."

Alyssum nodded in agreement.

"Come on, girls. No dilly dallying," Caroline called back to them.

"Distract Mother while I purchase a dress," Alyssum whispered as they began walking.

"What color did you choose?"

"Scarlet." Alyssum smiled happily.

"We're all going to be ruined." Violet shook her head.

"Oh, what about this color?" Caroline asked her daughters excitedly as they stood in the dress shop.

"It's beautiful," Violet said, looking at the turquoise material. She felt Alyssum tap her back, signaling that it was time. With a deep breath, she stood before her mother, blocking Alyssum from her view. "Perhaps we could ask if they already have a dress made in the color, then we could see what it would look like?"

"Splendid idea. Where did that seamstress run off to?" Caroline looked around. "Where is Alyssum?"

"Oh, she's probably getting some fresh air. She misses the country already and we've only been in London for two days."

"Poor dear," Caroline sighed.

"Let us look at more designs. I saw more samples over here." Violet took hold of her mother's hand and dragged her away from the front counter.

"Are you sure about this, missy?" the seamstress asked, looking at Alyssum with a stern gaze.

"Positive." She reached into her reticule and fished out the coins for the scarlet dress that sat in a white box on the counter before her. She had seen the dress on a mannequin near the rear of the shop. It had been waiting for its owner—a courtesan—but with some bribing, Alyssum had persuaded the seamstress to give it to her. Watching the seamstress tie a bow around the box slowly and carefully, Alyssum began fidgeting. She took quick looks around for any sign of Violet or her mother, or anyone familiar.

After the seamstress tied the bow on the box, Alyssum moved to take it. The seamstress didn't let go of the box.

"This dress was not made for a lady like you," she said.

Alyssum pulled the box from the woman's tight grip, handed her the coins and left the shop as quickly as possible.

Once on the street, Alyssum took a deep breath and exhaled. She had done it. She had bought the gown she needed and she hadn't been caught. She sighed deeply again in victory and prayed the dress fit.

"Alyssum!"

She jumped and spun towards the person that had called. Seeing Viscount Lambert approach, she fidgeted in fear as she held in her arms a daring scarlet gown that no proper lady should ever be caught wearing.

"Jumpy today, are we?" Robert pulled his hat from his head and stood before her. His wicked grin in place as he stared down at her.

"What do you want?" Alyssum asked abruptly.

Robert laughed and shook his head at her sharp tone. She was always like this with him, but it never deterred him. "I saw you and thought I would say hello."

"Well, hello." Alyssum shifted on her feet.

"Hello," he replied.

Alyssum shifted her gaze from his smile and down to his neck. She frowned at his low-hanging cravat. She sighed with irritation. Did the man not know how to tie a straight knot?

Tucking the box under her arm, she grabbed the lapel of his coat with one hand and pulled him down. Robert remained still and allowed her to retie his cravat with a grin on his face the whole time.

"Couldn't help yourself?" he muttered quietly to her as she finished. He tried to see her deep emerald eyes but her bonnet

29

hid them from him. He found himself disappointed he couldn't see her eyes.

Alyssum looked up then took a quick step back, placing the proper distance between them.

Robert smiled inwardly when she moved away from him like a skittish mouse. "Where's your chaperon?" he asked, looking around quieting street.

"Mother and Violet are inside." As the last words left Alyssum's mouth Violet and Caroline exited the dress shop with a jingling of the doorbell.

"Robert," Caroline called happily as she spotted him.

"Countess." He took her hand and placed a gallant kiss upon her knuckles.

"Rascal." She laughed.

Robert gave her a wink and turned his gaze to Violet. Violet huffed with such theatrics it made him laugh and she turned her face away and presented him her gloved hand. He took her offered hand and kissed her white glove. After releasing her, he stepped back and looked to the three beautiful women before him.

"Here you are, Alyssum," Caroline said. "We were looking for you in the store." Her gaze lowered to the box under her arm. "You purchased a dress?"

"Umm." Alyssum tightened her grip around the box and looked to Violet for help.

"Robert, are you enjoying London?" Violet distracted them all.

Robert's brow creased as he noticed Violet taking their attention away from the box in Alyssum's grip. He shrugged it off, thinking Alyssum had bought some undergarments and was blushing about it.

"I'm enjoying it very much," he replied.

"I'm sure you're glad to be making more scandals," Alyssum muttered under her breath, but they all heard. Robert turned his gaze down to her.

"Alyssum," Caroline chided her quietly.

"Good afternoon, ladies." He gave them a small bow then placed his hat back on his head and turned and walked down the street.

"Alyssum, why do you have to be so rude to poor Robert?" Caroline asked.

"Poor," she sputtered. "The man's richer than us."

Caroline huffed and shook her head. "I'll never understand it. You two used to be best friends." She walked by Alyssum. "Come, girls, we still have lots to do."

Violet and Alyssum walked two steps behind her.

"Is that it?" Violet looked to the white square box under Alyssum's arm.

"Yes," Alyssum whispered.

"I thought you were going to have it made?"

"I was, but then I saw this on a mannequin near the back of the store and it was perfect."

"I hope it looks awful on you."

Alyssum smiled. Tightening her grip on the box, she continued following her mother from shop to shop.

That afternoon, Caroline sat exhausted in the parlor while embroidering. Violet was by the window reading a book of poetry and Alyssum...she was outside in the garden, lying in the grass.

Alyssum stretched her legs with a sigh. She wiggled her bare toes in the grass. Her shoes and stockings were by her side, along with her bonnet and her hair pins. She stretched her arms out, glorying in the feel of the sun against her face. Her long raven locks were spread about her head, the curls sinking into the green grass. Here, with her eyes closed, she could pretend she was back home in the country. She was at peace.

"Careful, you're going to freckle," a man's voice reached her through her haven. "Apparently, it's very unbecoming on a woman."

Alyssum groaned and remained still with her eyes closed. It was a nightmare, that's all. Robert wasn't here.

"Alyssum, can you hear me?" he called in a laughing tone. Suddenly the warm sun vanished.

With a tortured groan, she opened her eyes and sat up. She glared at Robert, who stood blocking the sun with his back.

"Why, why are you here?" she demanded.

"Your mother invited me to dinner."

She sighed and turned her gaze away from him. She pushed her heavy hair back from her face, knowing she must look completely unladylike. She returned her gaze to him as he suddenly sat on the grass beside her. Bright rays of sun warmed her again.

"Ahhh." Robert sighed as he dropped onto his back and placed his hands behind his head. "This is nice." He closed his eyes and settled into the grass.

Alyssum looked around the small, secluded garden. She looked to her bare feet then saw her clump of stockings and shoes beside her. She blushed in embarrassment and grabbed them. She shoved her stockings and hairpins in her bonnet then slipped into her shoes.

"Are you ready for the season?" Robert asked as he kept his eyes closed.

Alyssum turned her gaze down to him. "Yes."

"Ready for Lady Brook's Masquerade?" he asked with a twitch of his lips.

Alyssum felt her heart leap. He didn't know her plan. Everything was fine.

"Yes, I acquired my costume today," she answered calmly.

"What are you going as? Maybe I'll find you."

"You won't find me," she said.

Robert opened his eyes and gazed up at her. He felt himself grumble in annoyance. Alyssum was a pain in his ass with her stiff, proper demeanor, but did she have to be so beautiful. He practically had to catch his breath every time he was around her. It helped when she would snap at him, then he was too busy thinking of quips to stare at her. But now, with her long midnight hair shining in the sunlight, curling about her shoulders, it was hard to think. The sun made her face glow. She looked like she had just been tumbled thoroughly and was glowing from satisfaction.

With that shocking thought, he sat fast and patted the grass off his coat. He kept his gaze from her, knowing it wouldn't be a good idea to look at her. Sex and Alyssum were never allowed in the same frame of thought.

"Why won't I find you?" he asked as his eyes grew strained from not looking at her.

"Because." She shrugged.

Robert's lips parted to speak, but he shut them when Alyssum stood. He turned his gaze to her and stared up at her. He squinted against the setting sun.

"Will you save me a dance?" he asked with his blasé grin in place.

"No," she replied as she scooped up her bonnet then turned and walked back to the house.

Robert chuckled lightly. Alyssum was the only woman who had never fallen for his charm or smile. It frustrated him, made him doubt his charm sometimes, but he always reminded himself to be grateful. For if she did fall for his charm, if she ever swayed near him and turned her lips up to him, he feared he might not be able to resist her. He quickly shook these dangerous thoughts drifting through his head and stood from the grass. He dusted himself off and made his way to the house, telling himself firmly to keep his mind clear of his best friend's beautiful sister.

"Dinner was wonderful, thank you for the invitation." Robert leaned down and placed a kiss to Caroline's knuckles.

"You must come by and visit whenever you wish," she told him.

"I will." He nodded and turned to Violet. He grinned devilishly. Violet laughed and raised her hand to him. He placed a kiss to her knuckles then stood straight. He turned his gaze to Alyssum. He arched a brow, as if daring her to give him her hand. The four of them stood quietly by the door in the foyer. The butler held Robert's coat and hat in hand, waiting.

Robert remained waiting, standing before Alyssum. Violet leant over and nudged her.

Feeling her family's gaze on her, Alyssum raised her right hand to Robert. She kept her expression nonchalant, but on the inside her stomach fluttered wildly. She wasn't wearing her gloves. His mouth would touch her skin. She felt her cheeks warming at the thought and prayed it wasn't noticeable. *Why?* she cried silently. Why did she have to react to *this* man?

With a grin curving his lips, Robert reached out, took her hand...and shook it.

Violet smothered her laugh behind her hand. Alyssum stared at Robert with fire in her eyes.

With a broad, satisfied grin that he had gotten the last say, he released her hand and stepped over to the butler. He took his belongings from the young man and slipped into his coat. He turned and gave the ladies a sweeping bow. "'Til we meet again." He placed his hat atop his head and left the house. The butler shut the door behind him and quietly left the foyer. Caroline and Violet silently waited for Alyssum's outrage. It came quickly.

"That man," Alyssum snapped, her voice echoing in the entrance hall.

"All right, gentlemen." Robert stared at each of his friends around the tavern's table.

Richard, the Duke of Linkinshire sat on his right. At thirty, Richard was the oldest in the group and was called Duke by his friends. With black hair smoothed back and wearing fine clothing, he was the image of a perfect gentleman, and he was.

Tucker, the youngest at four and twenty, sat on Robert's left. Golden brown hair and dark brown eyes, he was the second son of an earl and was quite the ladies' man, or so he thought.

Jackson West sat before Robert. Jackson had entered society a few years back after striking it big in a gold mine. Now that he was richer than any duke, society welcomed him with open, greedy arms. With black hair and laughing blue eyes, Jackson captured every woman's attention and always took what was offered, and that was why all the mammas kept their daughters clear of him.

While Robert was the most reckless and daring in the group, Jackson was the rake, Tucker the joker and Duke the mature one that sat back and watched them get into strife with a big smile on his face. Harry, when he did join them, was always the sensible one who dragged Robert away from trouble. But they all knew after three tankards of ale Harry could be just as bad as the rest of them.

Robert placed his cards in the centre of the table and listened to their cries of anger.

"Blimey. Why do I bother?" Jackson snapped as Robert scooped the bounty into his hands.

"Another round, my lovely," Robert yelled to the buxom tavern wench who had been serving them.

"At least he's buying," Duke grumbled and reshuffled the cards.

"Stop your bellyaching. Here." Robert flicked him a coin. "Will this shut you up?"

Jackson and Tucker laughed as Duke picked up the coin and inspected it.

Staring at the coin, he hummed, "Maybe two more." He laughed as Robert chucked him two more.

"Here you go, gentleman." The barmaid placed the jug of ale in the middle of the table. She leaned over low, giving them all an eyeful of her open bodice. They all saw the display from the barmaid and knew it to be an invitation. Robert moved first and took what was offered by grabbing her around the waist and pulling her into his lap. The men laughed as she giggled. Robert lowered his gaze to hers and felt his world slow down. He watched as a lock of the barmaid's pinned-up hair fell loose and fell over one globe of her breasts. Robert stared at the raven lock but he didn't see the barmaid's black hair and creamy breast. He saw Alyssum's.

He shoved the barmaid away like she had burned him. He grabbed his cards from the table and kept his gaze on them. He could feel the frowns of his friends on him. They were all curious as to what had just happened.

The barmaid pouted in disappointment and made a noise of unhappiness.

When Robert didn't draw her back, Jackson made a move and crooked a finger to her. Her smile returned and she slinked over to him.

Robert exhaled in annoyance. He looked to the wench now sitting on Jackson's lap. Her long black hair had now fallen around her shoulders. He needed to keep to his blondes. Blondes with brown or blue eyes, never green eyes and never dark hair.

With a shake of his head, he focused back on his hand of cards.

"Lady Brook's annual masquerade is almost here." Tucker rubbed his hands together in anticipation. Every year the first ball of the season was Lady Brook's masquerade. She always had the first ball and it was always the best. It had been for the last thirty years. Everyone wanted an invitation and everyone who received one always attended.

Jackson rubbed the wench's thigh. "Come back later, dove." He patted her leg.

She pouted again but stood and walked back across the tavern.

"What are we thinking this year?" Jackson asked, crossing his arms on the table and leaning forward with eagerness.

Every year, at Lady Brook's masquerade the men made a wager.

"I'm thinking something sweet this year." Jackson grinned.

"Something innocent." Tucker leaned forward as well. Excitement lit his young eyes.

Robert grinned at his friends. "You want to risk a leg shackle?" he asked Tucker. "Or your father's wrath?"

Tucker shuddered at the mention of his father. "Come on, Robert. A wager," he pleaded.

Robert arched a brow. "All right. Lady Brook's ball. Steal a kiss from a young miss and bring back one of her garters."

Jackson, Duke and Tucker laughed, their eyes alight with interest and excitement.

"Done. How much?" Tucker asked eagerly.

Robert twisted his lips while deciding.

"Hundred pounds," Duke spoke.

"Duke," Robert said, sounding impressed.

Duke laughed. "I'm not that old, boys."

Jackson clapped his hands together. "Hundred pounds, steal a kiss from an innocent miss and bring back one of her garters. Without being leg shackled or earning Daddy's wrath." He looked to Tucker with a smile. Tucker shoved him and Jackson fell from his seat. He hit the floor with a thud and the men roared with laughter.

Chapter Three

Alyssum took a deep, courage-filled breath. Her black cloak hid her dress from onlookers. She sat in the carriage alone. Violet had gone ahead with Mother. Alyssum had pretended she couldn't find her gloves and Violet had suggested they go ahead and send the carriage back. Caroline had sputtered and shaken her head, saying she wasn't leaving Alyssum behind. But after lots of gentle persuasion, Caroline had gotten into the carriage with Violet and they'd made their way to Lady Brook's.

The black domino hid half of Alyssum's face as she stepped from the carriage. A strip of scarlet peaked out from around the hem of the cloak as she walked up the front steps. When she reached the entrance hall, she could hear the voices coming from within the ballroom.

"My lady, your cloak?" A servant held out his white gloved hands.

Alyssum reached up, untied the cloak and let it drop into the servant's hands. She heard the servant swallow. Her back was revealed. Shoulders exposed. The bodice dipped lower than proprieties' sake. The long midnight waves of her hair were unbound and slung over her shoulder. The silk of the scarlet skirt swished around her legs as she walked forward.

"That one." Tucker nodded to the young miss who just walk by them.

"Too snobby," Jackson muttered and then took a swig from

his champagne glass.

They were dressed in black. Black coats, black waistcoats, black shirts, black breeches, black cravats, black boots and black masks. They looked like the rakes they were.

Duke turned his gaze around the room. "I should mingle," he grumbled.

"Have fun, Duke." Tucker patted him on the shoulder.

Duke moved forward and into the swarm of colorful dresses.

"Bees to honey." Jackson laughed as the mammas and their daughters bombarded Duke.

"He's an unmarried duke, ripe for the picking." Jackson and Tucker turned their gazes to Robert behind them as he spoke.

"About time you showed up," Jackson said.

"Couldn't find my mask," he explained and then snatched a flute of champagne off a passing tray. His attire was the same as the others, a black mask shielding his identity.

"Have you two chosen?" He took a sip of the champagne.

"Rosy over there." Jackson nodded his head toward a miss wearing a dark pink gown.

"I wanted that one," Tucker grumbled.

Robert chuckled at his sulking face. "Plenty of others."

"But look at her. Her eyes rake over every man who passes her."

Robert turned his gaze to Jackson. "You picked the easiest looking."

"Of course. I want my hundred pounds." He smirked.

"Remember, *just* a kiss," Robert said firmly.

Tucker and Jackson both nodded.

"Found her," Tucker announced with a bright smile. "Lavender over there." He nodded to the woman giggling around a bunch of men.

"Your turn, Robert?" Jackson said.

"Did Duke pick his?"

"He didn't say. We'll just find out when we meet up on the balcony," Jackson said as his gaze scanned though the crowds.

"All right." Robert looked through crowd of smiling faces. "Who to choose?" he muttered, looking for blondes amongst the brightly lit ballroom. Flowers scented the air as they decorated the room.

A loud smash broke his search. Girls screamed as champagne splashed the hems of their gowns. A man bellowed in anger. A servant had walked straight into a gentleman and dropped his tray filled with champagne. The servant's gaze was fixed on something on the stairs as people fretted around him. Robert, Jackson and Tucker followed the servant's gaze to the stairs.

"Holy hell," Jackson breathed.

"Mine," Robert said firmly as his gaze was transfixed on the beauty on the stairs.

Alyssum slowly descended the stairs. *Please don't recognize me,* she prayed. She had wanted a quiet entrance. She hadn't even allowed the man at the door to announce her, but then the servant had to stare at her and not look where he was going. Now all eyes were on her. The musicians had even stopped playing to stare. She felt her stomach flutter in nervousness as she stepped off the staircase and onto the ballroom floor. Guests remained staring, whispers sounded, heads popped up through the crowd to get a better look at her.

"Music," Lady Brook shouted and clapped her hands.

The musicians shook themselves and began playing. The servants scurried to clean the mess of broken glasses and spilled champagne. The ballroom broke out into an excited buzz and the gentlemen flocked to Alyssum.

"My lady, you're ravishing," a man gushed.

"More beautiful than the night sky," another announced passionately.

"May I beg a dance?"

Alyssum took a small step back. She reminded herself this is what she wanted. She was going to have fun. She stepped forward to one masked gentleman and gave him her black-gloved hand.

He took it excitedly and led her to the dance floor.

"Better jump in or you might lose her." Tucker nudged Robert while watching the woman in scarlet dance with a gentleman.

"They can dance with her," Robert replied. "But her garter is mine."

Jackson chuckled. "Thought you didn't like dark beauties? You usually run from them like they're the plague."

"Yes, what is it about dark-haired women?" Tucker asked. "Do they scare you?" He laughed.

Robert shook his head. He looked away from the woman in scarlet. "Excuse me, boys. I have rounds to make."

"Ah, the life of a titled gentleman," Jackson said.

"Exactly." Robert smacked his hand on Jackson's shoulder as he passed him.

"Where is she?" Caroline looked through the crowd for her daughter. "She should be here. What if something happened? What if the carriage overturned?" she rambled.

Violet rubbed her arm soothingly. "She's fine. It's a large crowd and she probably can't find us."

"Perhaps." Caroline nodded.

"My favorite women in the world," a deep, pleasant voice reached them.

Caroline smiled as she looked over to Robert. "Robert, don't you look dashing."

"I can't hide from you, can I?" Robert took her hand and placed a kiss on it.

"A mask doesn't hide that grin," she replied with a knowing smile.

Robert's grin broadened. He turned to Violet and kissed her white glove.

"You look lovely." He looked over her light pink gown.

"Thank you," she said quietly.

"Where's Alyssum?" he asked, looking around.

"She's lost in the crowd," she replied behind her white, plain mask.

"We hope," Caroline muttered.

"We hope?" Robert turned his gaze to her.

"We arrived separately," she informed him behind her peacock mask.

"She's probably hiding from all the noise." He smiled. "You know how she hates crowds."

Caroline exhaled with a nod. "You are right. She's probably hiding somewhere quiet."

"Violet, may I have this dance?" He held out his hand.

Violet's eyes widened. She looked terrified.

"It's a waltz. I'll make sure I go slowly."

"Go on." Caroline nudged her.

Violet accepted his hand and let him lead her to the dance floor. She wasn't a good dancer. She usually trod all over her partners toes. They would leave the dance floor limping.

Robert swung Violet into his arms and began waltzing slowly. She kept her eyes on their feet and counted under her breath.

"It's okay. I won't let you fall on your backside." Robert chuckled.

"You really need to learn to curb your tongue," she said while still looking down.

"You sound like your sister."

"Well, my sister is a smart lady."

Robert laughed. He added pressure to her back with his hand and turned her. "Where is your sister?" he asked casually. Only he knew that while he had dressed for this ball he'd had the single-minded thought of finding Alyssum tonight. She had sounded so sure that he wouldn't find her, so now he was determined as ever to unveil her.

"Somewhere quiet," she answered.

"Violet," he said firmly.

"I don't know. She's amongst the crowd."

"What color is her dress and mask?"

Violet turned wrong and stepped onto his toes. "Sorry," she quickly apologized and looked up at him.

"It's all right. I wore my tough boots tonight knowing I would ask you to dance."

Violet grouched and moved her gaze back to their feet.

"What color is her dress, Violet?" he urged gently.

Violet nibbled her lip while looking down. She slowly answered, "She's wearing a light-blue dress and mask."

Robert nodded, feeling triumphant. He would find her. "Thank you. Your sister thinks I won't be able to find her, but I'm ready to prove her wrong."

Violet nodded while watching their dancing feet. "Good luck finding her," she muttered.

"Pardon?"

"I said good luck," she said louder.

"She'll be easy to find." He smiled. "The girl standing stiff backed near the wall in a blue mask and gown. No trouble at all."

"You have no idea," Violet whispered under her breath.

"Pardon?"

"Nothing. Just counting."

"Is Alyssum enjoying London or does she miss the country?" he asked while swirling her slowly around the crowded dance floor.

"Why don't you ask her yourself?" She glimpsed up at him.

"She's difficult to talk to."

Violet smiled. "Not to me she isn't."

"That's because she likes you," Robert muttered grudgingly.

Violet looked up at him again. She saw his usual grin was gone, replaced by a cheerless expression. She frowned in confusion. "You can't blame her for her anger towards you."

"What? I didn't do anything."

"You're the reason she was sent to Paris in the first place. You made her the lady she is today."

"No, a school in Paris did that to her."

"If the both of you had never tried to burn your house down, she wouldn't have been sent away."

"We didn't try to burn the house down," he muttered, remembering the fiery blaze, the shock and fear as the room had caught fire way too quickly. He remembered how he'd grabbed twelve-year-old Alyssum and jumped out the window to land in the hedges. The disapproving gaze of her father as he'd found them dirty, sweaty and leaves sticking to their clothing. That was the night Alyssum had been spanked for the last time. After that she had been shipped off and had come back four years later as a proper, stiff lady who regarded him with cold indifference.

Pushing Alyssum from his mind, he twirled Violet around the room slowly and changed the subject of conversation to the weather.

Alyssum stared up at the man she was waltzing with. She had been taught to waltz at age nine. Harry had been selected as Violet's partner while she had been stuck with Robert who had purposely kept treading on her toes. He had been surprised when she had just trod right back on his, harder. Their friendship had begun that morning.

Alyssum tried not cringe at how her dance partner practically drooled down her cleavage. This night wasn't going how Jaz had described. Filled with romance, seduction, light touches and stolen kisses. It was, however, going along the lines of leering gazes, groping hands and vulgar whispers.

After she finished her dance and escaped the clutches of her partner, she snuck out onto the balcony. She breathed in the fresh, cool air. She heard voices below in the gardens.

Turning, she walked over to the far edge of the balcony and hid in the shadows. She leaned her elbows on the rail and stared down at the ivy that grew over the stone. Even wearing this gown her night had ended the same as usual. Her, alone, in a quiet corner.

Robert looked over the crowded ballroom and saw Jackson grinning down at his Rosy. He turned his gaze and found Tucker leaning against a white column while stroking the back of his hand down Lavender's arm. She stared up at him, giggling and blushing.

Robert exhaled sharply. He needed to stop looking for Alyssum and go win his wager. He shifted his gaze, looking for the bold scarlet dress. He had spotted her throughout the night, constantly surrounded by gentlemen.

Walking through the room, he saw three red dresses but none belonging to Scarlet.

He walked out onto the balcony but he found it empty. Just as he was about to turn and go back inside, he spotted a woman in the corner, hiding in the shadows. His eyes slowly adjusted to the dark and he saw her leaning against the railing. It was Scarlet. With another quick look around for any signs of guests, he walked over to her. As he made his way over, he stripped off his gloves and tucked them into the inside of his coat pocket.

Alyssum heard the footsteps of someone approaching her. By the clomp of the shoes on the balcony, she knew it was a gentleman. Hoping it wasn't one of the men she had already met tonight, she slowly stood straight but kept her back to him. She held the railing with her gloved hands.

The gentleman stopped behind her. She held her breath.

47

His shoes scuffed the stone floor then she felt the brush of his coat against her back. She exhaled and found her breath shook.

Alyssum gasped under the soft caress of fingers on her exposed back. She felt her skin tingling and responding. She remained still, wanting his touch. Her cheeks burned at her wicked behavior. She felt the gentleman step closer, his coat brushing her bare back. She then felt his warm breath at her ear.

The man raised both hands and smoothed them over her shoulders slowly, as if he didn't want to frighten her. He gently swiped her hair over one shoulder, dragging the waves behind her ear then across her neck.

Alyssum exhaled on a gasp as she felt his mouth touch her neck. His hands were warm and gentle as one rested on her shoulder and the other held her nape lightly. His lips were soft and firm as he led a trail of kisses up her neck. Her eyes drifted shut as his tongue swept over her skin. She felt her stomach somersault. Her breath shook with each draw of breath she took. She gasped again with a mixture of shock and pleasure as he began to gently suck her neck. She felt a change in her body. Her skin became sensitive to his every touch. She became hot. Her dress was too tight. Her breaths became heavier as she felt an ache begin between her thighs. His fingers at her nape stroked as his mouth sucked. Alyssum gasped for breath now. She had never felt these sensations before. She wanted more. She needed to touch him, feel him. She ached with want.

Robert felt her yielding to his touch. He had to be careful not to scare her away. She may have dressed provocatively, but every young lady in that ballroom was a proper miss. Lady Brook didn't invite harpies to her balls. Only the toast of the ton were invited.

He took hold of her arms and turned her around to face him. She arched her back and her breasts pressed against his chest. He stared down at her parted lips. He could hardly see her in the shadows, so he felt. He lowered his head and kissed the curve of her jaw, then her cheek, then the corner of her lip. Her breath fanned his lips before he fused their mouths together softly. He skimmed his hands along the softness of her cheeks and cupped her face. He tilted her head and slanted his mouth over hers. He seized her mouth in a hot, wet kiss. With her lips already parted, he thrust his tongue inside the warmth of her mouth and tasted her.

The kiss started slow and gentle, but with each passing second he felt the change in his Scarlet. She was no longer the innocent, but was now the eager student. He gave her his tongue and she suckled it. He groaned in pleasure. His breathing became heavier as the kiss spun out of control. His hands slipped from her face, captured her hips and brought her against him. He couldn't get enough of this woman. Where had she been hiding? She was incredible. This woman was his dream. Fiery, aggressive and addictive. His slid his hands down and grabbed her buttocks. He pulled her forward and ground her against his hardened shaft. She gasped and fueled his passion.

Alyssum gripped her masked man's coat in her fists. She kissed him hungrily, even wildly.

She felt a rush of heat sweep over her body. Her deep moans caused him to kiss her harder, deeper, so she moaned again and again.

She could hardly believe what she was doing, but it felt too good to stop. She couldn't pull away, wouldn't.

In her eagerness for him, she reached up and grasped the

back of his neck. She rubbed her body against him and couldn't stop the moans of pleasure rising within her. This was what she had come for. This perfect kiss. This perfect embrace. Body afire with passion, she clutched her masked gentleman and refused to let go. She loved the feel of his strong, hard body against her. She loved his mouth, his kiss, his touch. He grasped her buttocks in his hands and rocked her against the hard length of him. She squealed in surprised but wasn't afraid. With exhilaration racing through her veins, she pushed against him, wanting to feel every inch of him.

He grasped her ribcage and maneuvered her back against the wall. When her back pressed into the wall and her gentleman pressed into her, she knew heaven was real. He ran his hands up her ribcage then cupped her breasts. She scraped her teeth over his bottom lip with a whimper as he fondled her breasts. His thumbs brushed over her nipples and she shuddered. Suddenly, he ended the kiss. His hands remained on her breasts and his thumbs continued teasing her nipples. He kissed her cheek, making her sigh slowly.

"Who are you?" he asked, shaking his head as if amazed at his find.

Alyssum smiled. "Like I would tell you," she whispered. Her heart was pounding and her cheeks were burning.

Her hands still held the back of his neck, clutching him.

Robert could feel her silk gloves stroking his skin. He tried to identify her voice. She didn't sound familiar. Her voice was breathless and husky.

"What's your name?" He stroked her cheeks.

He saw her pause, felt her body stiffen against him. He felt he was about to lose her. Acting quickly, he leaned down and fused their mouths together in a deep, plundering kiss that made her gasp and grip his neck tightly. Tasting her sweet lips and feeling her tongue tangle with his, he groaned loudly and pushed his body flush against hers. He moved his hips against hers. He grinned against her lips as he listened to her deep, rapturous groans.

Shaking off the spell she had cast on him, he reached down and swept her leg up over his waist.

He pushed her skirts up and aside then glided his hand along her outer thigh. His hand touched her garter. With skilled fingers, he swept it down her leg. His mouth distracted her from his theft. Kissing her ravenously, he slid her garter over her shoe at his back, tugged it free and he shoved it into the pocket of his breeches. He glided his palm back up her leg as he moved his mouth from her lips to her neck. He listened to her frantic gasps for breath as he sucked fervently on her skin and caressed her thigh.

The sound of a gong ringing caused them to part. They both stumbled away from one another and looked at the open balcony doors. Cheers came from within the ballroom.

"It's midnight," she breathed shakily.

Everyone was revealing themselves and celebrating the beginning of the season. Robert turned his gaze back to Scarlet. He wanted her real name. He had to know who she was. He wanted her as his. Stepping towards her again, he saw her gaze flicker to his mouth before he tunneled his hands into her thick, curly hair and brought his mouth back to hers in a gentle but firm kiss.

Alyssum sighed and kissed her masked gentleman one last time. The kiss was slow and lingering. She glided her hands up his chest. She didn't want to let him go, she wanted to keep kissing him forever. But it was midnight and everyone was revealed. Masks were gone and she needed to leave. She smoothed her hands over his cheeks, memorizing the feel of him then stepped back.

"Who are you?" her gentleman asked. His voice was rough.

Alyssum frowned with uncertainty. She wanted a husband, someone to love her and cherish her. She doubted this man was he. Yes, he made her body burn as it never had before, but this man had embraced her, had kissed her knowing she was a lady. He was a rake, a scoundrel. He was no prince charming. She couldn't give him her identity.

Alyssum shook her head and began untangling herself from his embrace. She felt his reluctance to release her, but when she gently shoved his arms he let her go.

She took a step for the balcony doors. He suddenly stepped before her, blocking her path.

She stared up at her mystery man. He was dressed from head to foot in black and she could hardly see him, but she knew the feel of his hands...and his lips. She would never forget them.

"Please move," she said more firmly, her body regaining its equilibrium.

Robert frowned. He stiffened as her commanding voice reminded him of Alyssum. He shook his head at the preposterous thought. This woman before him *was not* Alyssum.

She may have the same gorgeous midnight hair but that was it. If he kissed Alyssum or even dared to rub his body against hers she would scream in outrage and slap him. Then Harry would have to kill him. He watched as his Scarlet fisted her hands. He grinned, curious to see what she would do.

"If I reveal myself, will you tell me who you are?" He stepped closer to her, moving her back against the railing.

She stared up at him for a long moment then Robert watched as she nodded faintly, hesitantly. He raised his hand, grabbed his black mask and pulled it off, revealing his identity. His hair now disheveled, he dropped his hand to his side, holding the mask and staring down at her, waited.

He saw no recognition light her features as he revealed his identity. For some reason that confounded him and he found he was nervous. He stood waiting for some kind of reaction from her. Maybe she didn't know him. He doubted it. His name was everywhere. Not being able to wait any longer to know the identity of his Scarlet, he took a step toward her and reached for her mask. She slapped his hands away, hard. He frowned and reached again. She side-stepped him and began making her way past him. She was trying to escape him. His hand whipped out and caught her before she could run. He swung her back around and reached for her mask with a newfound determination.

Dread caused Alyssum's heart to race. She felt Robert's hand at her mask.

Robert's. After years of playing cards with Harry, she had learned how to hide her expressions. Right now, as she looked up at Robert, her mind screamed in denial. But the truth was before her.

Robert. She had kissed *Robert.* Her neighbor. The boy who used to throw mud at her and drop frogs down her dress. The man she had just kissed and wanted to kiss again. *Robert.*

She couldn't allow him to find out it was she behind the mask. She couldn't bear to see his expression of horror when he found out that he had kissed her...and more. Remembering one of Harry's lessons in protecting her virtue, she raised her knee hard between his legs.

Robert hit the ground with a cry of agony.

Alyssum stared down at him in shock. She lowered her knee and watched as he squirmed on the floor, cupping himself between his legs. Turning, she quickly ran back into the ballroom and began making her escape.

Robert stayed down. Groaning in agony, he listened to the sound of Scarlet's feet run across the balcony.

She had kneed him. Right in the bollocks. He raised his head as he heard laughter.

"Guess you didn't get her garter," Tucker laughed as he and Jackson walked towards him.

"Saw your girl running through the ballroom." Jackson knelt beside Robert. "Are you doing all right?" He set his hand on Robert's back. "She kicked you in your treasures?"

"Yes," Robert snapped while clenching his jaw against the pain.

Tucker laughed and knelt down on the other side of him. "I guess we're all losing it," Tucker muttered.

"I haven't lost it." Jackson defended himself. "Rosy and I were doing just fine until I brought my tongue out and she slapped me."

Tucker laughed.

"Careful, that black eye is going to be more prominent tomorrow," Jackson warned him.

Tucker stopped laughing.

"You got hit as well?" Robert asked with a grimace.

"Jackson got slapped," Tucker pointed out.

"And Robert got kicked." Jackson smiled.

"What about Duke?"

"Too busy playing nice with the ton. He didn't even get a chance with all the mothers surrounding him," Jackson told Robert.

"So no one gets the hundred pounds." Tucker clapped his hands together.

Robert groaned and rose to his knees. He had planned to lie to his friends and say he hadn't obtained a garter. Not after having that passionate embrace with his Scarlet, but now, after that kick... Hell, he was getting his hundred pounds. Reaching into his pocket, he pulled out the black garter.

Chapter Four

The morning after Lady Brook's masquerade, Alyssum sat in the morning room with her mother and Violet, her gaze focused straight ahead at the wall beside Violet's head.

"Are you not hungry?" Violet asked, watching Alyssum.

Alyssum didn't answer. She was too busy staring at the wall and remembering Robert's kiss. With an audible swallow, she shifted her gaze from the wall and noticed Violet and her mother watching her with frowns.

With her fork midway to her mouth, her mother asked, "Are you well?"

Alyssum nodded, still unable to talk.

"Are you sure?" Violet asked.

She nodded again. Violet looked worried and glanced back down to her breakfast plate. Picking at a piece of ham, she shifted her gaze up to Alyssum.

Alyssum hadn't touched her breakfast. She sat with her hands in the lap of her light purple dress. She sat with her back straight, not a curl out of place, and stared with a faraway look.

"Sweetheart, should I call for the doctor?" Caroline asked.

"Alyssum?" Violet leant over the table and waved her hand before her sister's face.

Alyssum came out of her trance with a frown. "What is it, Violet?"

"You look like a ghost."

"I'll call the doctor." Caroline placed her cutlery down on

her plate.

"No," Alyssum quickly called before her mother stood. "I'm fine. The headache from last night still lingers, that's all."

"Such a pity you didn't stay at Lady Brook's longer. It was so lovely."

"It was beautiful," Alyssum agreed. "But I couldn't handle the crowd with my headache. I'm sorry I worried you."

"That's all right. I'm just glad you're well."

"Excuse me." Alyssum stood and then walked from the room. Caroline watched after her with frown.

"I'm going to go check on her." Violet stood.

"Yes, you should," Caroline agreed while staring at the empty doorway.

Violet left the room and ran after Alyssum. The skirts of her white dress swished around her legs as she dashed up the staircase.

"Alyssum," she called. Catching up to her on the stairs, she grabbed Alyssum's arm and stopped her. "What happened last night?" she whispered.

"What do you mean?"

"Alyssum, you tell me what happened or I'm going to Mother with the whole plan," she warned in a low voice. She saw Alyssum's eyes widen.

Alyssum looked around them. Violet did the same. Seeing no servants around, Alyssum leaned forward. "I got what I wanted," she said quietly.

"You got a kiss?" Violet whispered, her eyes wide.

"Yes," Alyssum mumbled, looking around.

"By whom?"

"I don't know." Alyssum cheeks flushed.

Violet frowned, noticing the blush. "Who?" she drawled.

"I don't know," Alyssum whispered with a snap.

"Yes, you do." Violet nodded while watching Alyssum's blush grow redder. "Who was it? It wasn't someone bad, was it?"

"Yes, it was," Alyssum gushed out. "It was horrible, horrible, horrible. I never want to speak of last night again."

"All right." Violet nodded, but Alyssum could see her sister was not going to give up on finding out who the man was.

Alyssum quickly stepped up the last three steps and began walking down the hall to her room.

"How about a ride?" Violet called out.

Alyssum paused then slowly turned. She tilted her head, contemplating.

"A nice ride in the park," Violet coaxed.

Alyssum smiled then nodded. "That sounds perfect. Thank you."

"I'll meet you downstairs in fifteen minutes."

Alyssum nodded and walked the rest of the way to her room.

She closed the door behind her and let out a long breath. Raising her hand, she touched her lips. She closed her eyes and saw her mystery man in black kissing her. Her eyes opened in a flash before her mind showed him revealing himself as Robert. *Robert.* With an aggravated sigh, she pushed the thought of Lady Brook's ball from her mind and began making her way to her room to change into her riding dress. Riding always cheered her up. Nothing could upset her when she was galloping, but for now she would have to settle for a trot through Hyde Park. When she got home she would gallop over the family's estate.

She walked to the corner of her room and rang the bell,

calling Meg, her maid. She stood patiently, waiting. Her gaze turned to her wardrobe. Shoved at the back was a white box filled with a scarlet dress, black mask, black stockings, black gloves and one garter. Her brow creased as she remembered discovering one of her garters missing. She felt her cheeks heat as she remembered Robert grabbing her leg, his hand caressing over her thigh. Had he taken it? Did he have her garter?

Taking a deep, calming breath, she turned towards Meg as she walked into the bedroom.

"Yes, my lady?"

"My riding dress, please," she instructed Meg. Meg nodded and walked over to the wardrobe.

Shaking thoughts of Robert away, Alyssum decided that the kiss was nothing.

He probably hadn't even given the woman he had kissed on the balcony a second thought.

Life would go forth, her plans of having a family would continue and the night on the balcony would fade. All she had to do was stay away from Robert.

Sitting in his quiet study with the morning sun shining through the open window, Harry frowned at the letter he was holding. After rereading it again, he leaned back in his seat and shook his head. "He's finally lost it."

Leaning his elbow on his desk, he rested his chin on his fist and stared down at the letter Robert had sent him.

Harry,

I need your help. I think I'm in love. Save me.

Robert.

"The season has just begun," he muttered, exasperated.

"What?" Jaz asked as she stepped into his office.

"Robert's already gotten into trouble. I think," he muttered the last bit.

"What did he do?" She stepped up before his desk. Her hair was unbound and falling wildly about her as usual.

"He says he's fallen in love." He handed Jaz the letter and noticed the dirt under her nails as she took it from him. "What do you think?" he asked after she read it and handed it back.

"You should save him. He's your best friend and he needs your help. You should go."

Harry squinted his eyes up at his little sister. There she stood, her hair a mass of tangles. Her lady's maid was going to growl when she saw the mud on the hem of Jaz's white skirts.

"Are you trying to get rid of me?" he asked, suspicious.

"Of course not," she gushed.

Harry grumbled, not believing her. "I'm not leaving you here by yourself so you can get into mischief."

Jaz deflated. Harry smiled. "Get back to your lessons," he instructed.

"Stupid Paris, stupid life," she grumbled as she stomped from the room.

Harry chuckled as he watched Jaz leave. Left alone again, he reached over for a piece of paper, dipped his pen into the ink and began writing back to Robert.

Robert finished drinking the tankard of ale and then slammed the cup down on the table. Jackson and Tucker stared at him and exchanged a look.

"What?" Robert snapped over the loud crowd in the tavern.

Jackson began shaking his head when Tucker announced, "You're no fun anymore. It's been a week since you were kicked in the bollocks. You should be up and having fun again, but *no*, you get drunk, you grouch and grumble under your breath and then you fall asleep."

Jackson cleared his throat. "Why don't you go see Harry's family? They always cheer you up," he suggested.

"No," Robert grumbled. "I wrote to Harry three days ago. He should be here soon."

"Good, maybe he'll slap some sense into you," Jackson mumbled.

"More." Robert waved his empty cup to the barmaid. When she came strutting over, Robert didn't pay her any attention, didn't even look at her. She filled his cup and left. Jackson and Tucker exchanged another worried look. "Harry better get here quick," Tucker muttered.

"What?" Robert snapped.

"I said Harry better get here quick," Tucker yelled across the table to him. "You bumbling tosspot."

Robert grouched then drank another cup. Tucker and Jackson rolled their eyes and slouched in their seats. It was going to be another boring night of watching Robert get foxed then carrying him home. Jackson didn't know who the woman Robert called Scarlet was, but if he ever met her he had some words to say to her. Whatever she had done, she had broken his friend. The man wasn't himself. He didn't smile. He didn't joke. He didn't pinch the barmaids anymore. Jackson didn't like what was happening to his friend.

At two in the morning in the quiet streets of London, Jackson and Tucker took Robert home, Jackson grunting under Robert's weight. Their friend was foxed to the gills, singing a tune that didn't exist and was slung over Jackson's shoulder.

Tucker opened the gate to Robert's townhouse and Jackson stumbled up the steps.

"Easy." Tucker held his hands out behind them.

"I got him," Jackson grunted.

"'E got me," Robert slurred.

"Shut up, Lambert." Jackson slammed his fist on the front door. A minute later, the old butler opened the door, unsurprised to see his master slung over Jackson's shoulder. Otis waved them in. Jackson walked into the house and up the staircase. His knees lowered with each step under Robert's weight. Finally reaching the top of the staircase, Jackson turned right and walked to the end of the hall. Tucker quickly reached around them and opened the door wide.

He threw Robert onto the large bed where he bounced, grumbled and fell asleep. Tucker and Jackson moved in, removing his boots, cravat and vest. Otis walked around them, carefully picking up the items of clothing that had been thrown around the room.

Tucker pulled Robert's shirt open and Jackson rolled him over to pull it from his body. As Robert rolled onto his stomach Tucker and Jackson both shifted their gazes away from his scarred back. Throwing the shirt behind them, they stepped back and chucked the corner of the quilt over him. Otis picked up the discarded shirt.

"When is Harry getting here?" Tucker whispered.

"Gentlemen," Otis spoke up behind them. They both turned and faced the butler. "There was a message delivered from the Earl of Leighton today," he informed them.

"What? Give it to me." Jackson held out his hand.

"Ah." Otis looked to his unconscious master.

"Come on, man, we haven't got all day."

The butler scurried from the room to retrieve the letter.

"We kind of do have all day," Tucker muttered, standing beside Jackson.

Jackson turned his gaze to Tucker and with one shove pushed him to the floor.

"Hey," Tucker whined but stayed down. At two in the morning, they were both exhausted. Tucker settled on the plush rug before the bed and closed his eyes as Jackson sat himself in a seat by the window. Otis, the gray-haired butler, scurried back in holding the letter, handed it to Jackson, bowed and then left.

Jackson tore open the letter and read. "What?" he snapped and read it again.

Robert,

It's time you saved yourself. My felicitations on falling in love.

Harry.

"You're in love?" He looked to Robert's sleeping form. "You don't even know her. You call the woman Scarlet because you don't know her real name. You spent less than five minutes with her," he argued.

"Will you be quiet," Tucker grumbled and rolled over to his side.

Jackson sighed and slouched deeper in his seat. He placed the letter on the small table beside him. "We men are going to find this Scarlet," he vowed for the sanity of his friend.

Violet took another glance at Alyssum. Her worry grew stronger. Now a week after Lady Brook's masquerade, Alyssum was acting stranger. Quieter, more withdrawn, she always seemed to be keeping herself busy or staring into space.

Violet had once again tried to get the name of the gentleman who had kissed her, but Alyssum had become angry and even more tightlipped. Whoever the man was, he had ruffled Alyssum's feathers worse than Robert ever had.

As she sat on the window seat in the front parlor, occasionally glancing out the window to the passing carriages, she took another look at Alyssum and frowned at what she saw. There Alyssum sat with a faraway look and her fingertips lightly touching her lips.

"Alyssum?" she called and watched Alyssum jump in her seat.

"Yes?" She looked to Violet.

"Have you heard anything from Jaz?"

Alyssum smiled and nodded. "She has written that she hates Paris, she hates us, she hates the grey, itchy uniform she has to wear and that when she comes back she's going to cause more havoc than she ever did before."

"Oh, my." Caroline rested her embroidery on her lap and looked up at Alyssum.

"Perhaps we shouldn't have sent her."

"She has only been there for a few days. Give her time."

"What were you like when you first got there?" Violet asked, curious.

"Quiet. I was terrified to be away from home and with a group of girls I didn't know. And most of them spoke French, so I had no idea what any of them were saying."

Violet chuckled and raised the book of poetry Robert had given her. Because she was a woman, she wasn't allowed to read most poetry that intrigued her. She wasn't even allowed in the stores where she could purchase them, so Robert bought them for her.

While half-reading the book, she took quick peeks at Alyssum. She needed to see some life in her sister again, some color in her cheeks. Knowing the perfect way to accomplish that, she lowered the book to her lap and turned to her mother. "Perhaps we should invite Robert to dine with us this evening?"

Caroline looked up with a smile. "Wonderful idea. I'll write to him now. Maybe he can get Alyssum talking again." She chuckled as she stood and walked over to the small writing table.

Violet smiled at the horrified expression on Alyssum's face. It was already working. Raising her book, she read happily.

Don't panic. Don't scream. Don't run away, Alyssum told herself. *Act calm, poised, composed. It's only Robert. Just annoying, unbearable, great-kisser, delectable-body Robert.* Alyssum groaned in ire. It was only a matter of time before she saw him again. He was almost a part of the family, there was no escaping that.

The clock ticked too loudly for Alyssum to handle. Her hands were clenched together in her blue gown. She sat on the settee beside her mother while Violet sat reading before the fire.

"Maybe he isn't coming," Alyssum broke the silence. "He's twenty minutes late."

"He said he was coming," Caroline answered with a frown of annoyance at Robert's tardiness. Dinner was getting cold.

"He's usually on time." Violet lowered her book and turned to face them.

"Maybe he forgot," Alyssum said. "Something may have distracted him..." Her stomach felt suddenly ill at the thought. Something distracting him...a woman?

"Alyssum, are you all right?" Violet asked as she stood and walked over to a suddenly pale Alyssum. Alyssum nodded but felt like she wanted to be sick. She had never cared what Robert did before now. Was he doing what he had done to her to another? She felt the settee shift as her mother stood with a huff.

"I'll send a message," Caroline said as she walked out of the room.

Alyssum hardly heard her, her mind was busy torturing her. "Stupid kiss," she muttered with anger, before she realized that Violet stood before her.

Violet opened her mouth to ask why she was thinking about a kiss when a sudden noise in the foyer stopped her. Both she and Alyssum walked across the room towards the entrance hall. The noise grew louder with each step. They both stood shocked at the sight of Harry holding up a drunken Robert.

"What happened?" Caroline gushed, looked up to an angry Harry. "When did you arrive?"

"Just now." Harry grunted and straightened a swaying Robert. "I found him on the front stairs."

"Such a good fellow," Robert muttered while trying to stay on his feet. His hair was a disheveled mess, his cravat was slung around his neck untied and his waistcoat hung open.

"Up the stairs," Harry ordered.

Robert turned and then tilted his head to look up the staircase. He turned back to Harry with a laugh. "Are you serious?" He pointed his thumb at the stairs behind him and laughed before he swayed off to the side and hit the floor. Harry rolled his eyes, Caroline gasped and Violet bit her lip, trying not to laugh. Alyssum stood stunned. Harry moved forward and grabbed Robert's arm. "Alyssum, help."

Her eyes widened. Violet nudged her forward with a push to her back. She moved perfunctorily and reached for Robert's other arm. She bent low beside Harry and they dragged Robert to his feet. He came up with a chuckle and slung his arms over both Harry and Alyssum's shoulders.

"Alyssum." Robert looked down at her with red eyes. She looked up at him reluctantly.

"Yes?" she asked in a crisp voice.

"Ah, I know that tone. Someone's mad." He grinned and leaned more into her. She grunted under his sudden weight and then sighed in relief as Harry pulled him back towards him, taking the weight off her.

"You know this girl used to walk through fire for me," Robert announced. "Literally," he shouted.

"Robert, quiet," Harry warned him. "Let's get you upstairs."

"No, I'm being serious." Robert leaned close to Harry to whisper, "I saw it."

Alyssum stood quietly by Robert's side with an arm around his waist. She had no idea what he was rambling about but she was getting infuriated with how her body was responding to his close proximity. She felt annoyingly happier by his side. His arm held her shoulder and his body kept swaying and bumping against hers.

"Alyssum?" he whispered and leaned back towards her. His face close to hers, he whispered, "Should I tell them?"

"Tell them what?" she said, confused.

"That you lit the match." He grinned.

Alyssum frowned before realization struck her. "You are drunk and I advise you to keep your mouth shut," she snapped. She watched with irritation as he grinned and turned back to Harry.

"Harry," he whispered.

"Enough, Robert," Harry ordered. "Phillip," he called and the butler came into the foyer. "Take Alyssum's side and help me get him to the guest room."

Phillip nodded and came forward. He had no struggle holding onto Robert and pulling him up the staircase with Harry.

Alyssum watched utterly bemused as they took Robert upstairs. Violet stepped up beside her. "What was he talking about?" she stared at Alyssum.

"About what?" Alyssum asked while keeping her gaze on Robert swaying on the staircase.

"You lighting the match?" Violet arched her brow. "About fire."

"I have no idea," she replied in a formal, proper tone of voice and made her escape towards the dining room.

"What a mess," Caroline spoke quietly while she and her family ate in the well-lit dining room.

"What was he doing on the front steps?" Violet asked, looking to Harry who was digging into his dinner. He looked up, realizing the question was directed at him.

"Probably tripped on the stairs and was too drunk to get back up," he muttered. "Or maybe he walked here and was taking a rest."

Violet shook her head with a smile.

"Sweetheart, what are you doing here?" Caroline asked. "I'm glad you are here, please don't misunderstand me. But you said you wouldn't be attending this year's season."

"I got a letter from Mr. West moments after I had already

received one from Robert."

"What did they say?" Violet asked.

"They were of a private nature."

"Robert? Private?" She laughed.

Harry sighed then replied, "Robert isn't well."

Alyssum, who had been sitting quietly all during the meal, finally spoke. "What do you mean he isn't well?"

"I don't mean not well in health. I mean he's not well...in the heart."

"What does that mean?"

Harry muddled over his words until Alyssum snapped, "Just spit it out."

"He has informed me he is in love," he announced. The table went quiet. Shocked silence filled the room.

"Robert is in *love*?" Violet asked incredulously.

Alyssum felt herself grow numb. Robert was in love. With whom? Who was the little tart?

"With whom?" Violet asked.

Harry exhaled and leaned back in his chair. "That's where things become...difficult. He doesn't know who she is."

Alyssum frowned and slowly began to feel her heart beat faster. "Then how does he know he is in love with her?" she asked.

"I shouldn't be speaking of these matters with you—"

"Who's the girl, Harry?" Caroline spoke, demanding an answer.

"He doesn't know her name because he doesn't know her," he announced. "He met her at Lady Brook's masquerade. She wore a scarlet dress and now he believes he's in love with her."

Alyssum's heart jumped and her eyes widened. She was the

little tart. She wasn't sure if her mouth was hanging open, she hoped not. She feared to look at Violet who was gaping like a fish out of water.

"That woman in scarlet. I remember her," Caroline said. "She was stunning. She took the ball by a storm with her gown."

"So you saw her?" Harry asked.

"Everyone did."

"What? What?" Violet sputtered, obviously finding it hard to believe what Harry was saying. "So he doesn't know who the woman in scarlet was?"

"No, he just calls her Scarlet."

"So...because he is in love, he is getting pickled?" she asked.

Harry smiled. "He wrote to me telling me to save him." He shrugged his shoulders. "I told him to save himself."

"Then what are you doing here?" Alyssum asked, still not believing the conversation they were having. Had Robert kissed another woman in scarlet that night? Or was Harry really telling her that Robert was in love with her, or thought he was in love with her?

"I got a letter from Jackson telling me to get my arse," he stopped mid-speech, a blush heating his face as he noticed he'd sworn in front of his mother and sisters. Violet and Caroline smiled. Alyssum didn't care. She needed to know what was in that letter.

"So he said get your arse here?"

Harry swung his surprised gaze to her. "Liss," he chided her.

"And what else did he say?" she urged.

Harry shook his head. "It doesn't concern you."

"But it does," Violet gushed then closed her mouth.

Harry frowned at her.

"He's a part of the family and I'm worried for his health," she told him while shifting her gaze.

"That's very nice of you, but he'll be fine."

"Because you're here?" Alyssum asked.

"Because I'm here," Harry agreed. "I'll keep him from drinking his stupid sorrows and make sure he shaves before leaving the house again."

Harry shook his head as he remembered Robert's appearance. Even though he'd shrugged it off as unimportant when speaking to the girls, he was worried on the inside. Robert had never taken more than a physical interest in a woman. He liked what he saw, propositioned, spent the night or a few in their beds, and then he was gone. He always kept his grin. But this was different. He remembered Jackson's words.

Harry,

Get your arse to London. Robert needs your help. He's driving me and Tucker insane and we don't know how to help other than to get him drunk. Some woman he has named Scarlet, for he doesn't even know her real name, has him bewitched something fierce. I'm worried he's quite serious about this one. Harry, the man hasn't even touched or looked at another woman since meeting this scarlet woman. All he does is mope and sulk.

HELP US.

J

Robert lay with the world spinning around him. He felt the soft bed underneath him, pressing against his cheek. He held

71

the blanket in his hands to keep him from floating away.

Through his pounding headache, he heard a soft whisper of a sound. The sound of silk against bare skin. He then felt a soft flutter of air at his ear. "Wake up." A pair of soft lips kissed his ear then licked. His body shuddered. With an eager moan, he rolled over to grab his seductress.

He hit the bedroom floor with a bang "Blast," he muttered as he woozily sat up alone in the room.

"Are you all right?" Harry asked from the doorway while holding a tray.

Robert exhaled with a groan as he remembered the events of last night. He had received the countess's invitation, but before he could decline Jackson and Tucker had shoved on his waistcoat and coat and pushed him from his townhouse. He dimly remembered the stumbling journey on foot then seeing the front stairs and thinking he would take just a quick rest. The next thing he knew Harry was waking him.

A harsh beam of sunlight broke through the curtains and lit Harry in the doorway.

"I'm sorry."

"Of course you are," Harry said as he walked in and placed the tray of food down.

Harry sat on the bed and stared down at Robert sitting on the floor. "All right. Let's hear it."

Robert looked up.

"Scarlet," Harry said.

Robert groaned. "I don't know."

"You said you loved her."

"I said *I think* I love her."

"You met her at Lady Brook's ball?"

"Yes," Robert answered. "The men and myself had a wager going on."

"Of course you did," Harry muttered. "What was it this year?"

"A lady's garter...and a kiss."

"A kiss from an innocent? Her garter? Are you crazy?"

"We wanted a challenge."

"Climb a mountain. Do you know what could have happened if you were caught?"

"Yes." Robert rolled his eyes, feeling like a boy again being scolded by Harry's dad for getting them into strife. He was just glad Harry had grown up to be like his father. If Harry had been like Robert's, he would be lashing him right now.

"Did you get the garter?" Harry asked.

Robert laughed and reached into his pocket. He pulled out Scarlet's black garter and handed it to Harry.

Harry inspected it. "Looks expensive," he muttered, looking at the lace.

"Well, only the *crème de la crème* go to Lady Brook's."

"What were you doing there?"

"Ha ha, very funny."

Harry smiled and handed the garter back. Robert placed it back in his breast pocket where it had been since the night of the ball.

"You know you may be able to find out who bought that dress."

"What?" Robert asked.

"Visit the top seamstresses. They wouldn't forget making a dress like the one everyone's describing."

"Huh." Robert contemplated it.

"Or we could get the invitation list from Lady Brook," Jackson spoke from the doorway.

Robert and Harry looked over to him. Harry stood with a smile and shook Jackson's hand as he entered. "Good to see you again, Jackson."

"It's about time you got out of the country and visited civilization." Jackson grinned.

"I like the country," Harry said.

"It's boring."

"It's quiet. And you can get away with a lot of things there." Harry quirked his brow.

Jackson laughed and clapped Harry's shoulder. He then turned his gaze to Robert still sitting on the floor. "You look lovely, Lambert."

Robert groaned and brushed his comment aside.

"The invitation list?" Harry asked.

"We could go through the list and find the ladies that match Scarlet's description."

"There were many women there," Robert stated. "It would take forever."

"Not as long as you may think. Plus, that dress she was wearing was something. I bet whoever made that dress would surely remember it."

"We don't have the dress to show them. Besides, Harry already suggested that."

"You know, your skepticism isn't helping," Jackson said.

"Just describe it. From what I've heard about the lady's gown, it was quite memorable," Harry said.

"Quite," Jackson scoffed. "Try very. I'm sure every man imagined his mistress to be Scarlet that night."

"Hey," Robert snapped and Jackson put his hands up in peace.

"Where's Tucker?" Harry asked.

"His daddy has him on a leash today," Jackson answered.

Harry laughed. "Poor Tucker."

"His loss. All right, plans." Jackson clapped his hands together and Robert winced at the loud noise.

"I will get the list from Lady Brook."

"Why you?" Harry cut in.

"Because I'm the most charming." He smiled his devilishly handsome grin that a lot of girls had lost their virtue to and Harry and Robert rolled their eyes.

"Harry, you clean Robert up."

"I don't need help." Robert began to stand. When the world spun he sat back down on the floor.

"Uh huh." Jackson nodded and turned his gaze to Harry. "We'll meet up at The Dove for dinner."

Harry and Robert were silent for a moment after Jackson left the room.

"Who put him in charge?" Robert grouched.

As Jackson walked down the hall of the Rosewood home, he paused when he came to an open doorway. Looking in, he found Violet sitting on a window seat with a book in her lap. He looked at her serene profile and then ran his gaze over her prim white dress.

"Morning, Violet," he put on his deep, roguish voice and grinned while leaning against the doorframe.

"It's Lady Rosewood to you, Mr. West," she replied without taking her eyes from her book.

He laughed softly when she didn't start blushing and stuttering like the rest of the innocent misses he met. "How are you this fine morning?" he asked in a casual voice.

"I'm well," she replied with her eyes still on her book. "How is Robert?"

Jackson shrugged in answer.

Sitting with her feet up and her back against the wall of the window seat, Violet waited for Jackson's answer to her question. When she didn't hear his reply after a moment, she looked away from the book in her lap and over to the door.

"Well, how is he?"

Jackson shrugged again.

"Is that an I don't know?"

Jackson chuckled and then nodded. "Yes, that's an I don't know."

"You could have said so," she replied and looked back down to the book.

Jackson moved to enter the room but a hard voice stopped him.

"What do you think you are doing?" Alyssum snapped at Jackson as she found him entering her sister's room.

"Alyssum." Jackson nodded to her with a smile.

"You think to enter my sister's room?" she spoke in an icier tone.

Violet whistled low and Jackson looked over to her. "You've done it now," Violet muttered.

"I was just saying hello," Jackson told Alyssum as she glared up at him. "It was all very innocent."

"Innocent would have been waiting in the parlor until she came to speak to you, *not* visiting her in her bedroom."

"I didn't," he defended himself. "I'm standing in the hall." He spread his arms out, indicating around him as they stood in the hall.

"I saw you about to enter."

"Did you?" He squinted his eyes at her. "Or did you *think* you saw me about to enter her room?"

"I saw you," she said firmly. "Perhaps I should get Harry?" She arched a brow.

Jackson grinned and nodded. "You play dirty. I like that."

"Leave. Now."

Jackson gave a small bow and then looked over to Violet. "Next time you want me in your room, sweetheart, make sure your sister isn't home." He winked and walked past Alyssum and down the stairs into the foyer.

Chapter Five

Jackson slapped the parchment on the tavern table and Harry, Tucker and a freshly dressed Robert looked up.

"Good to see you looking good," Jackson said to Robert.

Robert raised his cup to him in a salute and then took a drink.

"What's this?" Tucker asked about the parchment as Jackson sat next to Harry.

Jackson answered while looking across the table at Robert. "It's the list of people who attended Lady Brook's masquerade."

"You actually got it?" Harry asked, clearly surprised.

"You doubted me?" Jackson placed a hand over his heart and looked hurt.

Tucker laughed and picked up the parchment. He unfolded it and lay it in the middle of the table. "That's a lot of names."

Jackson whistled and Harry, Robert and Tucker looked up at him. They watched as he waved over the dark-haired barmaid.

"What can I do for you, gents?" she asked eagerly and looked at Jackson.

"We need ink and a quill," he said.

She deflated but went and got what they needed.

"You broke her heart." Tucker shook his head at Jackson. "Getting that lovely girl's hopes up."

"Let's focus on the list."

Jackson looked up as the dark-haired barmaid came back and set the quill and ink down with a thud. She darted him a glare then strode away, obviously angry at his indifference in seeing her again.

When Jackson looked back down, Robert had already crossed all the men's names off the list.

"Are you sure?" Jackson asked with a grin.

Harry and Tucker laughed as Robert glared at him.

"I'm sure," he replied. "I had her body against mine, she's female."

"Just checking," Jackson replied with an amused smile.

"Back to the list," Harry said, drawing their attention to the parchment and not each other's throats. Even though they were great friends, Robert and Jackson had gotten into a few brawls. It was how they had met. They had wanted the same barmaid. After the bloody brawl ended they had gotten to their feet, shaken hands and decided to get a drink. They had forgotten all about the barmaid.

Robert crossed off all the married women.

"Are you sure?" Harry asked with a frown.

"Scarlet's an innocent," Robert replied.

Harry nodded then watched Robert cross off the matrons. They all sat back once the list was narrowed down.

"Now what?" Tucker asked.

"Now it gets a little trickier," Harry answered.

"No, it won't," Robert said. "I know her body, her feel, her kiss. I'll find her." A smile then curved his lips and his heart leaped in excitement at finding Scarlet.

"Lady Jocelyn Williams," Harry read from the list.

"She's blonde," Tucker said.

Robert put the quill to her name and slashed over it.

"Lady Pamela Carrington," Tucker read from the list, his voice drawling with his boredom. They had been doing this for the past half hour.

Robert tilted his head as he contemplated. "I don't think I remember her."

"So it may be her," Jackson said, rushing him. He was just as bored as Tucker.

"She does have black hair," Harry said as he leaned his cheek on his fist.

Robert nodded and then continued down the list. He smiled then read, "Lady Violet Rosewood."

The men perked up at the familiar name.

"No," Harry said firmly.

"Now wait a minute," Jackson said with a grin. "Could she be Scarlet?"

"No," Harry repeated.

Robert laughed. "Don't worry, it's not her. Violet has brown hair." He slashed her name off the list. His pen then stopped and hovered over another familiar name.

"Alyssum." He stared at her name neatly written on the page.

"Now it's getting interesting." Jackson leaned back in.

"Once again—" Harry glared at Jackson, "—no."

"She does have black hair," Tucker said. "She's very beautiful."

"Tread carefully." Harry pointed to him in warning.

Jackson grinned. "What do you say, Robert?"

Robert looked up from the list. He slowly shook his head. "No." He forced a laugh.

"You say you felt her body," Jackson said. "Felt her kiss."

Robert gave him the same glare Harry was giving him.

"Come on, you told me Scarlet was a handful." He winked. "What size is Alyssum?"

Jackson grunted as he was hit from the side. He landed on the tavern floor with a thud and Harry got two good punches in before he was pulled away.

Jackson laughed and wiped the blood from his mouth. He sat up and found Robert and Tucker still sitting at the table. It was Duke holding Harry back.

"Good to see you again, Harry," Duke said as he held Harry's arm in case he went for Jackson again.

"You too, Duke."

"Keeping the boys in line I see." Duke smiled.

Alyssum stared at her closed bedroom door then looked back to the mirror before her.

Dressed in the scarlet gown, she ran her hands over the silk. With her long hair unbound, black curls ran down her back and over her chest. Closing her eyes, she felt herself back on the balcony and back in Robert's arms. She sighed and opened her eyes.

What was she thinking? *You don't want Robert*, she told herself sternly. Then why did she feel like crying at the thought of never kissing him again?

When a loud knock came to her door, she gasped and spun around, looking for an escape.

"Alyssum?" Harry called.

"Just a minute," she called back as she pulled the gown

from her body. Running over to her bed, she shoved the dress beneath it and grabbed her robe. As she walked to the door, she tied the robe tightly around her, hiding the fact that she was naked beneath it.

"Yes?" she asked Harry, slightly out of breath as she opened the door.

"Can I speak to you for a moment?"

"Ah," She looked behind her. Seeing her room was clear of evidence linking her with Scarlet, she opened the door wide and waved him in. "What would you like to speak to me about?" She turned and faced him. She frowned as Harry looked to be lost for words.

"What's wrong? Is Robert—?"

"He's fine," he waved her worry away. "Much better."

"Good," She nodded and became poised again.

"I wish to speak to you about Lady Brook's masquerade."

He knows. "Really? Why?" She fought to act calm.

"Mother told me you only attended for a few minutes and then left with a headache."

"Yes."

"So you never saw this Scarlet woman?"

Stay calm. "No. It was very crowded I could hardly find anyone in the crowd."

"You didn't see Lilly?"

Lilly. Perfect. "Actually I did," she said. "I spoke to her for moment before I left."

"Ah." Harry nodded. "So she saw you, wearing...?"

"A blue gown. Why are you asking me these questions?" she demanded.

Harry shook his head. "No reason. I just missed the most

popular event of the year and wanted to know what happened that night."

Alyssum nodded. "If that's all?" she said after a moments silence.

"Yes." Harry stepped past, heading for the door. "Sleep well," he said before leaving the room and closing the door. Alyssum frowned after him and then turned her gaze to under her bed. She gave herself a mental note to visit Lilly tomorrow. She needed her friend to do a huge favor for her.

As Harry stood outside Alyssum's bedroom door, he felt something wasn't right. He and the others had gone over the list bit by bit and had eliminated most of the ladies. There were now only five ladies on the list. One of them was Scarlet. But what unsettled him was that Alyssum was on that list too. With a sigh Harry stepped away from Alyssum's door and walked towards his own bedroom.

"I'm here to see Lilly." Alyssum smiled at the Darrel's butler.

"Come in, my lady. I will go inform Miss Darrel that you are here."

"Thank you." Alyssum walked past him and straight over to the parlor, not bothering to be escorted. She had visited often enough that she felt she didn't need to live by the laws of society.

Sitting down on the white settee, she folded her hands in her pink gown and waited. Lilly walked in a moment later. Her black hair was bound, her white dress straight, not a wrinkle in place. Lilly and her parents had come from America with big money from her father's perfume business. The ton had welcomed them, but still treated them like lower class behind their backs. It was why Lilly's parents were strict with her. She always had to look perfect, was never allowed to have a hair out of place, never allowed to slouch, always had to hold her pinky out when drinking her tea. She had to act the perfect English miss. Only Alyssum knew how much she hated it.

"I'm glad you're here," Lilly gushed before grabbing Alyssum's hands and pulling her up off the settee. She led her out the room, down the hall and through the glass doors. They stepped out onto the terrace but Lilly didn't stop there. She took them down the stairs, around a hedge before coming to a stop with a happy sigh.

"Are you well?" Alyssum asked with an amused smile as they stood in the quiet garden.

"I'm well, just suffocating under the watchful eye of Rickton." Lilly shuddered.

Alyssum smiled, knowing the familiar name of Lilly's chaperon. Old and strict, she was like a hawk watching its prey, and her prey was every man that approached Lilly.

With a loud sigh, Lilly dropped down onto the grass and sprawled out.

"Your parents would kill you if they saw what you were doing to that gown," Alyssum said.

Lilly laughed then sat. She patted the grass beside her and Alyssum sat beside her.

"I need a favor." Alyssum turned her head and looked at Lilly.

"Anything." Lilly nodded, her brown eyes staring at Alyssum with love and loyalty.

"I have a feeling Harry may ask you a few questions about me and Lady Brook's masquerade."

"But you weren't there. I looked for you."

"I was there," Alyssum admitted with a meek expression.

Lilly frowned.

"I was wearing a scarlet gown."

Lilly's eyes slowly widened. "You?" she breathed.

"Me." Alyssum nodded.

Lilly squealed and shuffled closer. "You have to tell me everything," she demanded with eager eyes. "Where did you get that gown? Why? How?"

Alyssum laughed at her excitement. "I bought it. Violet helped me. It was Jaz's idea."

Lilly shook her head. "Trusting that little demon."

Alyssum gasped and nudged Lilly's shoulder at Jaz's defense.

"Alyssum, why?" Lilly asked seriously.

"I wanted to have fun."

Lilly remained quiet then nodded. "I can understand that. Did you have fun?" Lilly laughed as Alyssum blushed. "My, my, what have you been up to, Alyssum?"

"I'll tell you everything if you promise me something."

"Done." Lilly gave a curt nod.

"If Harry asks you anything about me and the masquerade tell him we spoke for a moment before I left with a headache."

"Okay."

"And I was wearing a blue gown."

"Too easy. Now give me the gossip." She leaned in.

Alyssum took a deep breath then announced, "I kissed Robert."

"Pardon?"

"Robert, Viscount Lambert."

"Holy hell," Lilly breathed with widening eyes.

"Lilly!" Alyssum scolded her.

"You kissed Viscount Lambert?"

"Yes."

"How was it?" Lilly whispered.

Alyssum's blush burned brighter.

"I see." Lilly nodded with a smile. "And what does he think of all this?"

"He doesn't know."

"Pardon?"

"He doesn't know who I am. We were wearing masks."

"Then how do you know it was he?"

"He took his off."

"He didn't want to know who you were?"

"Ah, yes, but...I stopped him."

"How did you stop him?" Lilly asked curiously.

"I kneed him."

"Kneed him? Where?"

Alyssum cleared her throat then looked down to Lilly's lap.

Lilly looked down, then up and back down. With a gasp and wide eyes, she laughed. "You kicked his bollocks?"

"Lilly!" she covered her friend's mouth with her hand.

Lilly brushed her hand away with a laugh. "He doesn't know he kissed you?"

"No, and I want it to stay that way."

"Your secret is safe with me."

"I know."

"People are talking about the woman who was wearing scarlet."

"I know. I've heard the talk. It'll die down soon."

Lilly face twisted in thought. "So Viscount Lambert wanted to know who you were so much that you had to knee him?"

"Yes," Alyssum slowly answered.

"Do you think he'll look for you?"

Alyssum looked to her hands. "I think he's already looking."

Lilly's eyes widened in excitement.

"And I think Harry is helping." Alyssum looked up to her.

"Liss, you've gotten yourself into a pickle."

Alyssum nodded in agreement. They were silent for a moment before Lilly asked, "Do you ever think of seeing him again?"

"How do you mean?"

"As the woman in scarlet."

Alyssum began shaking her head. "It would be a bad, bad idea."

"But lots of fun." Lilly arched a brow with grin.

"It's a bad idea."

"Alyssum, do you want to kiss Robert again?"

Alyssum hesitated with her answer. "Yes," she admitted.

"Then see him again. Just wear the mask."

Alyssum couldn't believe it, but she was contemplating Lilly's idea.

Chapter Six

Lady Pamela Carrington.

Lady Lisa Knight.

Miss Lilly Darrel.

Lady Katherine Jenkins.

Lady Alyssum Rosewood.

Those were the names that rested in Robert's breast pocket. One of them was Scarlet. She had to be. As he walked into the Earl of Hopehill's *soirée* his thoughts ran to the earl's daughter, Lady Pamela Carrington. As he reached the top of the line, he bowed his head to the earl's wife then the earl himself.

"Good of you to come, Viscount Lambert," Hopehill spoke.

"Thank you for the invitation into your lovely home." He saw Hopehill's conceited wife smile happily at his compliment.

He moved past them and into the gathering of people. He ambled around the room, looking for Harry. When he spotted his friend, he walked through the crowd, ignoring the people who tried to grab his attention.

He felt the list in his breast pocket burn as he spotted Alyssum beside Harry. As always, she looked beautiful. Her green gown was respectable for society's eyes. Not a curl was out of place from her coiffure. His gaze moved to the lady beside her. Miss Lilly Darrel. He felt his heart beat faster as he stared at two of the women on his list.

"Robert," Harry greeted him. He noticed Alyssum stiffen at his name.

"Harry. Alyssum." He nodded curtly to her. She gave a small bob instead of a full curtsey. He couldn't help but smile at her. "And Miss Darrel." He bowed his head to her.

"Viscount Lambert." She curtseyed low. Robert frowned at her sultry voice. When she looked back up at him, she wore a mischievous grin. Robert's heart jumped at the possibility he had just found his Scarlet. He felt himself fearing the notion instead of rejoicing. Miss Darrel was lovely, but his gaze kept shifting to the lady beside her—Alyssum.

"Excuse us, ladies," Harry said then nudged Robert to follow him.

Robert took a step back while still looking at Lilly curiously. Could she be Scarlet? His gaze landed on Alyssum before he turned and followed Harry into the card room.

He spotted Tucker, Jackson and Duke in the room, overlooking a game.

"You ready, Lambert?" Jackson grinned with a lip bruised from Harry's fist.

"Lilly Darrel," Robert said, after making sure no one could eavesdrop on their conversation.

"The American, what about her?" Jackson frowned.

"She grinned at me."

"*Ooo*, scary," Tucker laughed.

"She was acting out of character," Harry said.

"You think she's Scarlet?" Duke asked casually. He had been nonchalant and unconcerned about Robert finding his Scarlet.

Robert shrugged.

"He doesn't seem very excited about the prospect," Tucker muttered to Jackson.

"I'm going to go find out." Robert turned around and

walked back into the crush of people with a determined march. The others watched him leave.

"He won't cause a scene, will he?" Duke asked, now standing to full attention.

They all pondered Duke's question and then moved as one to follow Robert.

"Miss Darrel."

Lilly turned as her name was spoken. She tried to hide her knowing grin as she raised her chin to look up at Robert. "Viscount Lambert." She curtsied.

"May I have this dance?" he asked, ignoring the other women that were around her.

She looked around and spotted Rickton watching her with squinting eyes.

"I would be honored." She offered him her hand. He took it and led her to the dance floor.

She stood in line with the rest of the ladies dancing and smiled as Robert stood across from her with the other men. He stared at her so intently, as if trying to solve a problem.

As the dance began, they both moved in together.

"Did you attend Lady Brook's masquerade?" he asked as he took her hand and they circled.

Lilly felt her eyes widen. He wasn't even going to start with light chatter. The man was on a mission. Before she could reply, they moved apart. Lilly was ready when they came together again. "Of course I did. I wore a stunning green gown my father purchased for me."

Robert felt himself relaxing. He didn't understand it, but he was happy that this wasn't his Scarlet. She was still out there to be found.

"Did you enjoy yourself?" he asked.

"Yes. And it was good to see Alyssum. I hadn't seen her in months while she was in the country."

"You saw Alyssum?" Robert tried not to growl in annoyance as the dance moved them apart.

When they came together, she answered, "Yes, only for a moment though, she had a headache and left early."

"Could you tell me the color of her gown that night?"

Lilly smiled sweetly at him. She took his hands and they turned. "Why don't you ask her yourself?" She fluttered her lashes, trying to look the innocent.

Before he could push her for more information the dance ended and they stepped back into their lines. Robert bowed low as she curtsied. They clapped lightly to the musicians and Robert stepped forward and took her waiting, outstretched hand. He led her back the group he had taken her from and the ladies fluttered their fans, hiding their smiles as he approached.

"Thank you for the dance." Robert placed a kiss on her knuckles and stepped back.

"My pleasure," she replied.

He bowed curtly, ready to move away, but his eyes caught on a lady with midnight-black hair. Pamela Carrington.

"Lady Carrington." He bowed to her.

She preened at his acknowledgment and lowered her fan. "Viscount Lambert." She curtseyed low, giving him a view of her cleavage.

Robert overlooked her display. "May I have this dance?"

"It would be my pleasure." She gave him her hand.

Lilly watched Viscount Lambert and Lady Carrington walk out onto the dance floor before she looked around the room for Alyssum. Instead she spotted Harry with his cronies. Her brow creased as she noticed them watching Robert dance with Lady Carrington intently. They watched his every move.

"*Hmm*," she hummed in interest. She excused herself from the group and walked around the dance floor to reach Harry. On the way, her gaze caught on Alyssum standing beside Violet.

Alyssum watched the dancers while holding a glass of punch. Lilly noticed that she shifted her gaze away from the dancing couples as Lady Carrington's laughter filled the dance floor.

Lilly moved with purpose as she rounded the room. He stood with his back to her. She reached up, uncaring of watchful gazes, and tugged on the back of his coat.

Harry turned quickly to see who had tugged on his coat. He looked down and a bright smile curved his lips as he saw a friendly face.

"Lilly." He bowed.

"Hello, Harry. I was just curious as to why all you gentlemen are watching Viscount Lambert in such an...intent way." She looked at each of the men who now watched her.

"And how would you know we were watching him?" Jackson stepped forward and asked.

Lilly kept her chin high as she looked up at the infamous Mr. West. She had been warned about him. "I have eyes," she replied tartly.

"So were those pretty eyes watching Robert or Harry?" He arched a brow.

"Maybe they were watching you." She arched her brow back at him.

Jackson found himself smiling at the brazen minx before him.

"Miss Darrel," a stern, whip-lashing voice broke their gaze.

Lilly groaned before turning her gaze to Rickton. Grey hair pulled back tight, stern lips twisted in disapproval and a grey itchy-looking gown, Rickton flicked her hand towards her, indicating for Lilly to come with her. Lilly took a deep breath then faced the men before her. She curtseyed and then strode over to Miss Rickton.

"I'm going to get some air. It's really crowded in here," Alyssum told Violet.

"Okay," Violet replied, but Alyssum was already heading for the terrace doors.

Outside in the cool air, Alyssum took a deep breath. Her chest had hurt as she had watched Robert hold Lady Carrington, dancing with her, making her laugh.

Needing to be far away she strode down the stairs quickly and walked over the grass. She walked behind the rows of hedges. No longer able to see the house, she dropped down and lay out on the grass. The skirts of her green gown fanned out. She could hear the distant music and laughter. She sighed and looked up at the black sky. She missed the country. When she lay beneath the night sky at her family's country estate she could see the stars. Seeing something so beautiful usually washed away her anger. Now, with no stars in the sky, she only wanted to go back in time, stand on Lady Brook's balcony and knee Robert again.

She sat bolt straight as she heard a giggle over on the other side of the hedge.

Oh, please no. Please, please—

"Viscount Lambert, you naughty man," Lady Pamela Carrington gushed.

Alyssum closed her eyes and groaned quietly.

"This will only take a moment and then I'll get you back inside," Robert's clipped voice reached her.

Alyssum snorted in an unladylike manner. *Only a moment?* He had spent longer than a moment with her. Two or three at least. Alyssum stood with a huff as she heard Pamela giggle.

"You are a skilled kisser," Pamela breathed.

Alyssum rolled her eyes. "Tart," she muttered under her breath.

"Let's get you back inside," Robert said.

"No, let's stay here," Pamela urged.

Alyssum waited, almost pressing her ear to the prickly hedge to hear Robert's reply.

"I'm going inside," Robert said offhandedly. "You can stay out here if you want."

Alyssum felt a smile tug her lips as she heard his footsteps and Pamela's huff of outrage. Pamela stomped over the grass as she returned to the *soirée*. Alyssum dusted off her dress and waited a few minutes before making her return.

Robert walked straight over to Harry and the others when he reentered the gathering.

"Report?" Tucker ordered then laughed. He lightly swayed on his feet and Duke grabbed his arm and held him steady. Robert arched a brow at Tucker's drunkenness.

"Not her," he informed them.

"So it's not Lilly and it's not Pamela," Harry said.

"Are you sure it's not Lilly?" Jackson asked. "She seems

like a minx under those prim clothes."

"I'm sure. When I was dancing with her she was too short to be Scarlet."

Jackson nodded. "And Pamela?"

Robert exhaled. "She wore a yellow gown to the masquerade." Pamela had been the easiest to question. She had had no problem talking about herself and what she had done that night at Lady's Brook's masquerade. She had been seductive though. In case she was toying with him, he had led her out into the gardens. She had scurried behind him in excitement. But he had felt nothing when his mouth had touched hers. She had kissed him back teasingly, wanting more. He had felt no heat, no passion in her kiss. His heart had not raced and he hadn't been overwhelmed with the urge to have her. She was not his Scarlet.

"So we keep looking for this mysterious woman?" Duke asked, still holding Tucker upright.

Robert exhaled and looked over the crowd. His gaze caught on midnight black hair and a green gown. Alyssum. He felt his heart jump at the sight of her. He cleared his throat, paying no attention to his reaction to her.

"Excuse me, gentlemen." He nodded to them and moved away, heading for Alyssum. But as he nudged by the group, a hand clamped onto his upper arm and pulled him to a stop.

Robert turned with a frown. He looked down to his restrained arm and then up to Harry who held him. "Yes, Harry?"

Harry must have seen which lady Robert's gaze was on. "Alyssum—" Harry nodded in her direction, "—isn't your Scarlet. You remember that. She's my sister."

"I'm not going to forget that anytime soon." Robert patted Harry's hand and his friend released his grip. Harry stepped back but still watched him with a stern expression.

Robert cleared his throat before he spoke. He never liked having heartfelt conversations so he spoke quickly. "I would never harm Alyssum, or any member of your family." He then turned and walked across the room to Alyssum, feeling Harry's eyes on him as he went.

"Hello, beautiful."

Alyssum felt herself freeze. Turning slowly, she faced Robert. He grinned down at her.

She lowered her gaze to his cravat and quirked a brow at its straightness.

"I had my valet do it," he whispered to her as he noticed her attention on his cravat.

"You should always let him do it."

"But I like when you do it."

"What do you want?" she snapped.

Robert laughed and shook his head. After being miserably foxed for the last week he'd found himself missing Alyssum's sharp wit. "I'm saying hello," he answered.

Alyssum shifted her gaze around them as a few curious onlookers watched them.

"Well say it and leave."

"No. I find myself wanting more." His grin was back in place.

"What do you really want?" she demanded quietly.

"A dance." When Robert saw she was going to say no, he added, "I'll make a scene."

She glared. "You wouldn't."

"Oh, I would." He laughed. "Well?" He offered his black-gloved hand.

Alyssum stared down at it. She sighed deeply then slowly raised her hand.

Robert's grin disappeared, a smile taking its place. She was going to dance with him.

His hand reached farther, wanting to whisk her up quickly before she changed her mind. He was just about to grasp her hand when it was suddenly snatched away from him.

"Sorry to interrupt." Lilly smiled as she pulled Alyssum towards her. "But I must steal her away. Do forgive me, Viscount." She led them away through the lively crowd.

Robert fisted his hand then let it drop to his side limply. He exhaled. *So close.* Grabbing a glass of champagne from a servant's tray, he downed the contents then picked up another two. Holding the champagne glasses, he walked over to a smiling face.

"You'll be nice to me, won't you?" he asked Violet while handing her one of the glasses.

"Of course I will." She sipped her champagne as they stood side by side at the edge of the dance floor. Robert noticed Violet was watching the dancing couples quite wistfully.

"Would you like to dance?" he asked.

"Did you wear your strong boots?"

Robert chuckled. "I must beg forgiveness for I have forgotten to wear them."

"I'll find a way to forgive you." She smiled up at him then turned her gaze back to the waltzing couples. "I saw you speaking to Alyssum," she said casually.

"Yes, Lilly stole her away." He took a large gulp of champagne, emptying his glass.

"Ah." Violet nodded. "How's your Scarlet?"

Robert looked to her in surprise then, with an exhale, muttered, "Harry."

"He worries about you, that's all."

Robert grumbled in reply.

"Do you know who she is?" she asked calmly.

"No," he grouched. "But I will soon enough."

"Really?" she turned her eyes away from the graceful dancers and looked up at him. "Any ladies I might know?"

"Yes."

"Are you going to make me beg?"

Robert grinned at her. "I have a list," he whispered.

"Of what?"

"Possibilities. There are two more women on the list."

Violet's eyes widened. "Can I see it?"

Robert hummed.

"*Please*," she pleaded.

"Come with me." Robert nodded towards the terrace doors.

"If someone sees…"

"I'll keep you safe," he assured her with a wink.

"All right."

Robert took her glass and placed both their flutes on the table behind them. She took his offered elbow and allowed him to lead her out onto the terrace.

"Now he's got Violet," Alyssum muttered to Lilly as she watched Robert and Violet walk through the glass doors.

"He's looking for you, Liss," Lilly warned her. "He asked me about the masquerade. Even asked what color my gown was, then he asked what color yours was."

"What did you say?"

"I told him to ask you himself."

Alyssum smiled.

"I think I got him off your trail when I told him I had spoken to you before you left."

Alyssum nodded. "He would never believe it's me anyway."

"So he kissed Pamela Carrington?" Lilly asked.

"I heard it. She then *urged* him to stay outside with her."

"I knew she was a doxy," Lilly whispered and Alyssum smiled again.

At that moment, Lilly and Alyssum both looked behind them to check if Miss Rickton was still standing a good distance between them so she couldn't hear their conversation.

"Alyssum?"

"Yes?" She turned her gaze back to Lilly.

"Would it be so bad if he knew you were the woman he was searching for?"

Alyssum remained silent. She then answered quietly, "He would be horrified." She turned her gaze away before Lilly saw the sadness in her eyes. She still couldn't believe he had kissed Pamela. Why not her? Why didn't he try to steal her away into the garden? Why did he only come near her to vex her?

"Lady Pamela Carrington," Violet read the small list in her hand. She tilted the paper towards the window they stood before, hoping to catch more light. She squinted her eyes in the dark, trying to see the list clearly.

"I know it's not her." Robert stood with his back against the wall beside the window. His arms were crossed over his chest as he watched Violet read.

"How do you know?" She looked up to him.

"I just know." He shrugged.

"Hmm." Violet turned her gaze back to the list. It was hard reading it in the dark but she managed with the candlelight coming from inside.

"It's a small list. Are these guesses?"

"No, a friend managed to obtain the invitation list from the masquerade."

Violet turned her quizzical gaze back towards him. "It was Mr. West, wasn't it?"

Robert laughed then nodded.

"What did he have to do?"

"It's a secret," Robert whispered. Violet rolled her eyes skyward then turned her attention back to the list. Robert smiled down at her. If only she knew. Lady Brook was a faithful woman and had never betrayed her husband, but she did play games of chess with young gentlemen for favors. Jackson now met with her at her townhouse and played chess in her drawing room. He had nine more games left before the favor was complete.

"Is that Alyssum's name?" Violet asked.

"Oh, yes. Um," he stammered to explain. "She matches the description. The men wouldn't allow me to cross her off until I know for certain."

"Do you know for certain yet?" she asked casually while watching him.

Robert forced a laugh. "It's not Alyssum." The woman didn't even dance with him. Why the hell would she kiss him?

"So how do you find out these women aren't Scarlet?"

"That knowledge is unsuitable for your innocent ears."

"They're not that innocent," she muttered while handing the list back to him. "By the by, Katherine Jenkins just left town."

"Why?" he asked, not remembering having met the lady.

"Her sister is having a baby and she wanted to be there."

Robert sighed. "So that leaves Lisa Knight," he muttered.

"Until Miss Jenkins comes back. Have fun with your hunt." She patted his shoulder before leaving his side and walking back into the *soirée*.

Robert remained outside, listening to the buzzing crowd within the house. His thoughts drifted to Scarlet. He remembered her kiss, how innocent she had started then how passionately she had responded. She had rubbed her body against his, wanting him. His hand slipped into his coat pocket and touched the black garter. He would find her.

When Robert arrived at his townhouse after the ball, he walked straight to the library and poured himself a brandy. Leaning against the bar, he stared into the dying flames in the fireplace. After taking a swig from the glass, he placed the drink down and pulled out the list from his breast pocket. Walking over to the small table in the room, he grabbed the pen from the desk, dipped it into the ink and slashed two more names off the list.

Lisa Knight, she was next on his list. He would have to wait for Katherine Jenkins to return.

Robert placed the list back in his pocket then drained the rest of the glass. He worried over the fact that what bothered him the most about tonight was not that he didn't find Scarlet, but that Miss Darrel had stopped him from dancing with Alyssum.

Chapter Seven

When Alyssum woke in the morning, she felt excitement instead of dread. Robert was looking for her. Telling herself repeatedly that it was a bad, bad thing, she got herself ready for the day before her maid came to wake her.

Not bothering with breakfast, she gathered her tools and gloves and went straight to the garden out the back.

In the solace of her garden, she began relaxing, allowing all her worries to flee. She snipped a dead daisy from the bush and placed it in her basket. She continued to work happily, cutting away the dead flowers.

"Good morning," Robert's silken voice spoke behind her.

Her hand froze mid-reach for another dead flower. Her heart began beating wildly in her chest. Alyssum sighed at the loss of her calmness. As Robert walked closer to her, she heard his boots crunching over the grass. She turned her head and saw two black boots beside her.

"What brings you here, Viscount Lambert?"

"Viscount Lambert?" Robert sighed. "You'll never call me by my first name will you?" he asked as he stared down at her.

"Harry's still sleeping," she told him, still keeping her face averted.

Robert nodded at the information then sat beside her. Now facing her, he smiled as he saw her face.

"We didn't get a chance to dance last night," he told her.

"Such a shame."

"You'll break my heart if you keep being mean to me."

Alyssum fought to hide her smile then, with a huff, she sat back on her legs and looked at him. She felt her whole body freeze as his hand reached out and tucked a loose curl behind her ear. His fingertips left scalding prints on her skin.

"I thought your heart belonged to Scarlet." She mentally slapped herself.

Robert pulled back gently, lowering his hand. "You know about her?"

"The whole family does, and the ton is clucking like hens about the woman in scarlet."

Robert exhaled and leaned back on his hands. "What do you think about her?"

Alyssum shrugged and turned back to the daisies. "I don't think about her."

"Do you think about Mr. Potting?" he asked.

Alyssum turned her surprised gaze back to him. "Wh... I..." she stammered over her words.

Robert grinned and rendered her speechless. "Why did you want to marry the vicar anyway?"

"He was a nice man," she snapped.

"I know a lot of nice men. Would you like to marry them?"

Alyssum didn't answer, just chopped a flower harshly. "So this Scarlet woman..."

Robert exhaled.

"Do you love her?" Alyssum paused and faced him, waiting for his answer.

Robert shook his head. "I don't know her."

"But you're spending all your time looking for her."

"No, I'm not. When I have a spare minute I'll ask a question or two. I'm curious like all the others," he lied.

"What happens when you find her?"

"I don't know." He laughed.

"Well, what would you say?"

"I guess, hello."

"Hello?" she repeated. "You would just say hello? After searching all that time that's all you would say?"

"Sure."

Alyssum made a noise of distaste and began hacking the daisies, not even caring if the ones she cut were dead or alive.

"I don't know what the daisies did, but I'm sure they're very sorry they upset you."

Alyssum clenched her jaw. Grabbing another stem, she held her scissors clenched tight in her hand and snipped.

Robert must have seen her flinch and heard her quiet squeak. The scissors dropped onto the grass and Alyssum turned away, holding her hand.

"Let me see," Robert ordered and leaned over to try and grab her injured hand.

"It's nothing," she said tightly.

"Then show me."

Alyssum moved to get up but Robert grabbed her ankle through her skirts and pulled her sharply towards him. She gasped as she slid over the grass and stopped right before him. He let go of her ankle and grabbed her injured hand. She fought to get her hand back but he pulled the working glove from her fingers.

She stopped fighting once they both saw the blood. Raising her hand, Robert looked at her sliced index finger. He winced as her blood ran down her hand and dripped onto the grass.

"Does it hurt?" he asked when she didn't complain.

Alyssum shook her head quickly with a pained expression.

Robert laughed softly. "Liar." He moved closer to stare at the cut. "It's deep," he muttered. "You should call the doctor."

"I'm not going to call the doctor over a cut."

Robert stared at her blood running over her wrist then looked up to her. He arched his brow.

"I'm fine," she snapped and tugged on her hand but Robert didn't release her. He reached into his pocket and took out his handkerchief. Alyssum hissed against the pain as he wound the soft piece of cloth around her finger.

While holding her hand, he raised his other to tuck the same loose curl behind her ear again. Alyssum looked up with gasp as he touched her. A crease furrowed her brow as she stared at him. It was then she realized how close they were sitting together.

Her lips parted, her breath panting lightly she watched frozen as Robert reached up again and stroked her cheek with his thumb.

He looked into her wide green eyes and smiled at her shocked expression.

"Ahem," an amused voice reached them.

Alyssum shoved Robert's chest and pushed him back onto the grass. She stood fast and turned towards the voice. She sighed as she saw it was only Lilly smiling broadly.

"I didn't mean to interrupt," Lilly said sweetly with her hands behind her white skirts.

"Of course you didn't," Robert muttered as he pulled himself up and stood. He looked over to Alyssum and rubbed his chest where she had shoved.

Lilly chuckled quietly but then stopped and gasped as she

saw Alyssum's hand bleeding. "What happened?" She raced forward to grip Alyssum's hand and inspect it.

"I nicked my finger with the scissors."

"Nicked," Robert scoffed. "She sliced her finger. Make sure she calls the doctor."

Lilly unwound the handkerchief gently then gasped again as she saw the cut. "Alyssum, this is really deep."

"I'm fine," Alyssum snapped and took her hand back. She wound the handkerchief tightly and winced. Blood now seeped through the cloth. She stared at her blood as it came through the material and dripped down onto the grass. She raised her hand then watched as the blood trailed down her arm and seeped into the indent of her elbow.

"Liss, you're as white as a ghost." Lilly placed her arm on Alyssum's shoulder. She then grunted as Alyssum suddenly slumped against her unconscious.

"What did you do?" Violet cried as she saw Alyssum pale, unconscious and in Robert's arms.

"Me?" Robert snapped. "I didn't do anything. She sliced her finger while cutting the daisies and fainted at the blood."

"Blood." Violet suddenly stopped her approach towards them. She looked to Alyssum's hand then turned pale.

"Oh, not you, too," Robert pleaded.

"We...we Rosewoods...we don't do very well with blood," Violet said weakly.

"You don't say?"

"What's going on?" Harry demanded as he entered the parlor and saw Robert placing Alyssum down on the settee. He reached her side quickly and patted her cheek. "Alyssum?"

106

"She's out cold," Robert told him.

"What did you do?" demanded Harry.

"I didn't do anything."

"It wasn't him. I saw it happen," Lilly spoke up on the other side of the settee. "She fainted when she saw how much blood there was." She nodded to Alyssum's hand.

Harry looked at Alyssum's hand then blanched. "Violet, call the doctor."

Violet nodded and ran from the room.

Harry turned back to Alyssum. His gaze lowered to the seeping, red handkerchief around her finger. He took a step back and swallowed visibly.

"*No*," Robert breathed as he saw Harry going pale. "You've dealt with blood before."

"In fights," Harry replied. "I'm the one who hits them so I don't care if they bleed."

"Are you all right, Harry?" Lilly asked gently and placed a hand on his arm. "Maybe you should wait for the doctor outside?"

Harry nodded, seeming grateful for the escape. He turned and left the room quickly.

"Strange bunch," Robert said before looking back down to Alyssum. She lay pale as death. And the white settee wasn't helping her look any healthier.

"You don't get it do you?"

"What?" Robert looked to Lilly.

"Their father," she said and realization hit Robert in the chest like a sledge hammer.

The former Earl of Leighton had died in a riding accident. Tenants had found him and brought his body back to the

house. He had been broken and bloody. It had been Caroline
and Harry who had cleaned his body of the blood, but not
before Violet, Alyssum and Jasmine had seen the tenants
bringing their dead father up to the house, covered in dirt and
blood.

"I didn't even think about that."

"Well, they do," Lilly said quietly.

Robert looked down to Alyssum. He still remembered how
he had been the one to find her hiding in the woods after her
father's funeral. He had held her while she cried over his shirt.
He had never wanted to see her in such pain again.

Robert cleared his throat loudly. "I'll go check on Harry.
You stay with her."

"I think that would be proper." Her lips twitched as though
she was remembering the position she had found Alyssum and
Robert in out in the garden.

Robert saw her meaning in her smiling eyes. "Not a word,"
he whispered and pointed a warning finger at her.

She slashed a cross over her heart, swearing she wouldn't
say anything. Robert then turned and left the parlor.

Alyssum slowly opened her eyes. She looked around in
confusion. Where was she?

"Rise and shine, sleepy head." Lilly's face appeared above
her.

She pulled herself up then held the seat beneath her for
balance. "Why am I in the parlor?"

"Because you fainted. Viscount Lambert carried you in."

Alyssum hid her blush as she looked down at her injured
hand. "Urgh." She looked away from the blood.

"Here." Lilly stepped around the settee and sat down beside

her. She pulled out her own white square handkerchief from the reticule wrapped around her wrist and replaced the bloody one with it. Lilly stood and threw the soiled linen in the fireplace. "Is that a little better?"

Alyssum's lips pinched as she watched the new handkerchief turn red.

"Don't let her look at it."

Lilly and Alyssum turned their gazes to Robert standing in the doorway.

Seeing Alyssum's pale face, Robert moved forward and came to sit on the other side of Alyssum. She followed his gaze when he looked down at her hand.

"No." Robert captured her chin in his hand and made her look up at him. "Don't look down," he told her. He lowered his gaze while his grip remained on her chin. "Lilly, can you get a maid to get us some bandages and warm water?"

"Of course. I'll be back soon." She waggled her fingers and left. As she exited the room, she pulled the door almost closed. Alyssum was thankful Robert kept his back to the door and didn't see Lilly's improper behavior.

"How long will the doctor be?" she asked quietly. Her chin tilted as she tried to look down but Robert tightened his grip, keeping her chin up.

His laughing eyes met hers. "I said don't look down."

"It's my hand," she snapped. "If I want to look at it I will."

Robert laughed and Alyssum felt her stomach summersault as his thumb brushed over her jaw.

"Just keep your eyes on me," he instructed. "Most women don't have a problem with that." His grin turned into a smile when she rolled her eyes.

Robert turned his head around as he heard footsteps

outside the door. He reluctantly let his hand fall from her chin.

Alyssum felt like she could breathe again as his fingers left her skin.

"Alyssum?" They heard Violet's voice.

"Yes?" she called out.

Violet sighed at Alyssum's voice. "Are you well?" she asked, still outside the door.

"You can come in."

"Oh, that's all right." Violet waved the invitation away. "Lilly can keep you company while I wait for the doctor."

Robert turned his gaze back to Alyssum and arched a brow at being called Lilly.

"Oh," Violet said surprised.

The door then opened and revealed Lilly. She walked in with a maid behind her carrying the bandages and a bowl of warm water. Violet stood just outside the door. Her eyes widened slightly as she saw Robert sitting beside Alyssum quite closely on the settee.

Lilly took her former seat beside Alyssum while the maid placed the bandages and water on the table before them.

"Thank you, that will be all." Robert nodded to the maid.

She curtsied and left.

"What are you going to do?" Alyssum stared at the water suspiciously.

"The doctor's taking too long and we have to clean the wound."

"It is clean."

Robert smiled and took her injured hand. She snatched it back.

"Alyssum." He held his hand out, waiting for her to place

her fingers in his.

"I think he knows what he's doing," Lilly whispered in her ear from behind.

"I do," he assured them.

Alyssum sighed deeply then gave him her hand. He peeled away the blood-sodden handkerchief. He looked up quickly as she hissed in pain. When she nodded she was fine, he returned to her hand. Placing the linen on the table he picked up the bowl of warm water and sat it on his lap.

Alyssum looked up towards the doorway and found Violet gone. She returned her gaze to her hand and felt herself grow queasy as she saw fresh blood.

"I don't feel good," she whispered.

"Lilly, distract her," Robert muttered while he washed her finger in the warm water. The water turned red.

"How?"

"Talk to her." He pulled her finger from the water and inspected her wound, making sure no dirt was in the cut.

"Remember Lady Brook's masquerade," Lilly said suddenly. Both Robert and Alyssum turned their gazes to her. Robert's was one of curiosity while Alyssum's was wide with alarm.

"Remember the dancing?" Lilly asked with a nod.

"You danced?" Robert asked Alyssum. "I thought you didn't stay long."

"She stayed for dance or two, especially with all her admirers." Lilly smiled and Alyssum felt the room spinning around her. She felt herself growing queasier. What was Lilly doing? She wanted to silence her quickly but Robert's hand held her captive. She couldn't move while he was touching her gently. She winced and gasped as she felt a pinch of pain on her finger. Turning her gaze downward, she watched Robert wind a

111

strip of cloth around her finger firmly. Through the swirling haze of her dizziness, she heard Lilly still talking.

"Her beautiful blue gown... They flew to her like bees to a honey pot."

"Really?" Robert drawled.

"Robert," Alyssum breathed as she swayed on the settee.

She saw Robert's shocked gaze jump to hers a moment before everything went black.

While Alyssum lay unconscious in his arms for the second time this morning, Robert tied the bandage around her finger.

"Go get Harry. He can take her to her room," he told her and set the bowl of water on the table.

Lilly nodded and jumped to her feet. Robert watched her leave. Now alone, he turned his gaze down to Alyssum. She had said his name. It had been like a whisper, a caress over his skin. His whole body had reacted to her voice. He missed hearing his name on her lips. He missed her. Raising a hand, he smoothed the back of his fingers down her cheek. "Alyssum," he said quietly.

He removed his hand as he heard heavy footsteps coming this way. With a sigh, he lifted Alyssum in his arms and rose from the settee. Harry would have punched him if he walked in and had seen Alyssum lying over his lap.

"Is she okay?" Harry asked in a rush as he entered the room.

"She's fine. She just fainted again."

Harry nodded then took Alyssum into his arms. He held her high up against his chest.

"I'll help you take her to her room," Lilly said.

"Thank you." He turned and walked from the room with

Lilly walking behind him.

Robert remained standing in the parlor. He shook his head, clearing it. "Too much is happening," he muttered under his breath. First meeting Scarlet, now Alyssum calling him Robert. He looked out the window to check the sky wasn't falling.

When Alyssum woke it was to find an old man leaning over her. She screamed and sat bolt straight.

"Easy." He put his hands up, stepped back and chuckled.

"Alyssum, he's the doctor," Lilly spoke.

Alyssum turned her gaze towards her window and found Lilly sitting on her window seat.

She sighed. "Apologies," she told the doctor.

"No problem. Now that was quiet a slice on your finger. You keep it clean and I've left ointment for you. I want you to apply it to the cut every night."

Alyssum nodded and looked down to her bandaged finger.

"All right, you take care next time with those scissors."

"I will." She raised her gaze away from her bandaged finger.

The doctor left, taking with him his black case. Lilly stood from her seat on the window and came over to sit on the bed beside Alyssum.

"It has been an eventful morning."

Alyssum blew out her breath and nodded. She looked down and found herself only garbed in her white shift.

"Do you remember everything?" Lilly tilted her head to the side.

Alyssum nodded.

"Do you remember saying Robert's name before you fainted

for the second time?"

Alyssum gasped. "I didn't," she breathed.

"Oh, yes, you did." Lilly laughed. "You look more shocked than he did."

"He heard?"

"He heard, and I think he liked it as well." Lilly waggled her brows.

"Stop it." Alyssum smacked Lilly's shoulder and Lilly laughed.

"What I want to know is how you cut your finger?"

"I told you how, with the scissors."

"But you're always so careful."

Alyssum sighed then told her, "He made me mad."

Lilly chuckled.

"What did he say?" Lilly asked intrigued and leant forward.

"He said he's only looking for Scarlet because he's curious, just like the rest of society."

"What twaddle. He's looking for the woman who set his heart aflame," Lilly said passionately. "Who sparked his desires to a burning pitch!" She placed her fist over her heart and looked into the distance. "The one woman who has truly given him pleasure."

Alyssum chuckled lightly.

"I'm serious."

"The only woman who's given him pleasure?" Alyssum arched a brow, doubtful.

"Okay, so men these days aren't monks, but that doesn't mean you didn't give him something no woman ever has."

"And what would that be?"

"Love." Lilly smiled.

Alyssum stared at her for a moment before chuckling again.

"Hey," Lilly gasped.

"*That's* absolute twaddle."

"It is not. Where's your garter hmm?"

Alyssum stopped laughing.

"Why would he take it?"

Alyssum shrugged her shoulder, not knowing.

"My advice, tell him before he finds out himself."

Alyssum shook her head quickly.

"Yes. I saw you two in the garden," she said firmly, stopping Alyssum's head shaking. "If I hadn't interrupted he would have kissed you."

"No, he wouldn't have. He wants Scarlet."

"You are Scarlet," Lilly exclaimed.

"I was." Alyssum sighed. "Now I'm just Alyssum."

"So put that dress back on and be Scarlet."

Alyssum chewed her bottom lip.

"Where's the dress?" Lilly asked.

Alyssum's gaze moved to her wardrobe across the room in front of her. Lilly turned around and looked at the wardrobe then jumped from the bed and went over to begin searching.

Alyssum stepped from the bed. Her head no longer swayed with dizziness.

"It's at the back in a white box," she told Lilly and fidgeted on her bare feet.

"Ah-ha." Lilly dragged the white box out. She brought it over to the bed and placed it on the mattress. She pulled the lid off and they both looked into the box. Alyssum's heart fluttered while Lilly stared in awe.

115

Alyssum reached into the box and pulled out the scarlet dress.

"It's beautiful," Lilly whispered. She then turned her gaze back to the box and pulled out a black glove.

"You have to. How could you not?"

"Have to what?"

"Be Scarlet again."

Alyssum chewed her lips again. "I don't want to risk it. What if he pulls my mask off?"

"Then kiss him to distraction." Lilly laughed. "He'll love it, like he loves you."

"He loves Scarlet," Alyssum muttered.

Lilly placed the glove back in the box, walked around Alyssum, grabbed her shoulders and turned her towards the long mirror. Alyssum stared back at her reflection as she held the scarlet gown in her hands.

"Alyssum, I'm only going to tell you once," Lilly said sternly.

Alyssum looked up and caught gazes with Lilly.

"You are Scarlet," she told her firmly, leaving no room for argument.

"Not anymore." Alyssum shook her head and turned away from Lilly and the mirror.

She packed the dress away and tucked the box back into her wardrobe. Lilly stared at the closed wardrobe for a moment then looked to Alyssum.

"You should begin to get ready."

"Pardon?" Alyssum asked, confused.

"Remember we're going to the theatre tonight?"

Alyssum sighed and nodded.

"I'll see you tonight." Lilly waved before leaving.

Alyssum stood quietly in her room, her gaze on the wardrobe. She remembered how it felt to wear the dress, to feel Robert's kiss on her lips.

She turned with a huff, marched over to the bell pull and called her maid.

"I'm not Scarlet," she whispered to herself.

Chapter Eight

As Alyssum and her family were filing into their box at the theatre, her mother whispered at her ear, "Why didn't you wear the lavender gown?"

"It was wrinkled," she answered.

Caroline nodded with a smile and patted her arm.

"Are you feeling well?" Harry asked gently.

"I'm fine," she told him. They had been asking her all afternoon. She wore a pair of long white gloves, hiding the bandage around her finger.

"Well, this should be a wonderful evening," her mother announced.

"It should be."

Alyssum paused at the sound of Robert's voice behind her.

"I thought I would say hello before the play began," he said.

She turned to see him speaking to Caroline.

"That was sweet of you." Her mother smiled brightly up at him. As always, he placed a gallant kiss on her hand then Violet's. He looked over and their eyes met. She smiled hesitantly.

"Are you well?" he asked.

"She's fine," Harry, Violet and Caroline answered in unison.

"I see I'm not the only one who is concerned."

Concerned? Hoping her face wasn't blushing, she replied, "There's no need for concern. I'm fine and will continue to be so."

"Good." He smiled and her breath caught. "I'll see you all at intermission." He bowed and left the box.

She was finally able to breathe when the red curtain fell behind him as he left.

As the curtain lifted on the stage and the play began, Alyssum kept her eyes trained on the stage and tried not to think of Robert and the scarlet gown in her wardrobe, but she couldn't help it. She missed his kiss.

A quarter way through the play a surge of excitement and gasps ran through the theatre. Alyssum turned her gaze from the stage, trying to find out what had caused the stir. She felt her heart stop. She gasped. Scarlet.

Not realizing what she was doing, Alyssum stood from her seat and stepped toward the edge of the box. Down in the pit was a woman in a scarlet gown. She wore a black domino and black gloves. Alyssum shook her head, not believing her eyes. That was her dress.

"Oh my," her mother breathed behind her as she looked at the new Scarlet.

She felt Violet stand beside her. "But..." She also shook her head, not understanding.

"Who is that?" Violet demanded.

"Scarlet," Harry muttered the word everyone was whispering.

Robert was running. He dodged past couples and ran down the hall.

He knew Tucker and Jackson were helping. They had left the box as well to find her.

119

She was here. Scarlet. He had hardly believed it was her when he'd looked down and saw her, but there she was, scarlet gown, black gloves, black mask, long black hair. What made his heart pause was the fact that even though he was standing and ready to chase Scarlet his gaze had moved to the Rosewood box. His gaze had caught on Alyssum. She had been staring down at Scarlet with shock written all over her face.

He had then dragged himself out of the box and began running. He had to know who she was.

Lilly gasped as she ran. Her hands were bunched in the dress's skirt as she held it up and ran. The dress was way too long for her. It trailed behind her and she had to gather more in her hands. Seeing an alcove, she jumped inside and whipped the curtain closed. She moved back and gasped as she bumped into music stands. She heard heavy footsteps run past.

She placed her hand over her panting mouth. When silence filled the hall, she exhaled in relief and moved to leave the alcove. She poked her head out and looked up and down the empty hall. She tiptoed out and then began walking quickly.

A hand grabbed her arm and yanked her back against a hard chest. Her mouth opened, ready to scream, but a strong hand clamped over her mouth. She gasped against the man's palm.

"Hello, Scarlet," he breathed into her ear.

No, no, no. This wasn't how it was meant to happen.

"Let's see what you're hiding behind this mask."

As she felt his hands untying the bow at the back of her hair, she struggled in his grip. He grunted against her strength but kept hold of her. The mask came off and she was spun around in his arms. She heard him gasp. Too afraid to look up, she kept her head down until strong fingers gripped her chin and tilted her head back.

Her eyes widened as she stared, not into Robert's brown eyes, but Mr. Jackson West's blue gaze.

"Lilly?" he breathed.

"Please don't say a word," she gushed out.

He shoved her back. "You? You're Scarlet?"

Lilly was shocked by how much anger she saw in his expression. She shook her head. "I'm not Scarlet."

Jackson laughed and arched a brow at her dress. He then frowned as he looked closely at it. Lilly knew it was practically falling off her, and the Scarlet he had seen at Lady Brook's had fit into the dress with perfection.

"You're not her. But you know who is. You took the dress from her."

"Please, I beg you, don't say a word about this to *anyone.*"

Jackson's grin curved his lips. "You owe me one." He pulled his coat off and handed it to her.

"Better run before Robert finds you."

She took the coat and shrugged into it, wrapping it around the scarlet gown. Before she turned, his voice stopped her. "It's Alyssum isn't it?" he asked.

Lilly stared up at him in silence and he grinned broadly.

"Both your secrets are safe with me."

She sighed with relief and then smiled as she saw an easier way to finish her plan.

"Get Robert drunk tonight."

Jackson laughed and took a step toward her. "You want to run that by me one more time?"

"Which tavern do you frequent?" she asked and stared at him intently.

"The Dove," he answered.

"Take Robert there tonight, get him drunk but not too drunk, and I'll give him his real Scarlet for the night."

Jackson shook his head at her. "What are you planning?"

"My best friend's future happiness." She smiled brightly. "Now get him drunk and I'll send Alyssum at ten o'clock."

"Bit early."

"Not for a lady. Now do as you are told."

Jackson laughed and bowed his head to Lilly. When he looked back up it was to see her running down the hall. He watched her until she disappeared and then turned as he heard approaching footsteps. Realizing he still held the black mask, he shoved it into his pocket and stepped forward just as Robert rounded the corner.

"Did you see her?" Robert asked, panting.

"No." Jackson smacked Robert's shoulder. "Sorry."

Robert exhaled in defeat.

"Come on, let's watch the end of this boring play then get drunk at The Dove."

Robert followed him back to the box. Halfway back to their box, Robert frowned at Jackson. "Where's your coat?" he asked.

"I gave it to a pretty little thing," Jackson answered with a jaunty grin.

Robert chuckled.

Hours later Alyssum closed her bedroom door, leaned back against it, closed her eyes and exhaled.

"Please don't be mad," a quiet voice reached her.

Alyssum's eyes snapped open to find Lilly sitting on her bed beside the scarlet gown.

"You." She stepped forward.

"Please. I had good intentions." Lilly jumped up, her hands raised in surrender. No longer wearing the scarlet gown, she was garbed in one of her white dresses. Her hair was no longer unbound.

"What were you thinking?" Alyssum whispered angrily.

"That you would see sense."

"How?"

"Did you like seeing Robert running after another woman?" Lilly asked with her hands planted on her hips.

"He wasn't running after another woman. He was running after Scarlet."

"And who is Scarlet?"

"Me!"

"Ah-ha," Lilly exclaimed victoriously while Alyssum exhaled. "You are the woman he wants, so stop being difficult and go to him."

Alyssum's heart raced. She remembered the feel of his kiss on her lips, his body against hers. She nodded before she knew what she was doing.

"Really?" Lilly asked.

"Yes," Alyssum breathed.

Lilly squealed in excitement. "Okay, I have my carriage waiting outside—"

"What about your parents?"

"It's bridge night at the Harvey's and my jail warden's fast asleep," she replied.

Alyssum nodded and they both turned their gazes to the

dress.

"How did you get the dress?" Alyssum asked.

"Your butler let me in and I stole it. Now, Robert will be at The Dove and slightly drunk, so if he tries to take your mask off and you're not ready, a simple shove should put him on his backside."

Alyssum smiled and nodded. She was doing this. She was going to Robert.

"Oh, we have one slight problem."

"What?" Alyssum asked cautiously.

"Mr. West has the mask."

Alyssum stared wide eyed before shouting, "Mr. West? Why does Mr. West have my mask?"

"Shhh." Lilly looked to the closed door then back to Alyssum. "He has your mask because he took it."

"Lilly Darrel, you better start talking."

"All right." She held up her hands. After releasing a deep breath, she began, "Once I knew Viscount Lambert had seen me, I ran. I hid in an alcove for a minute but when I came out a man grabbed me." Lilly released another breath as she spoke quickly. "I was so scared, I thought it Robert. Then, while all these thoughts of how my plan was ruined were running through my head, he took the mask off and turned me around. It was Mr. West."

"I wouldn't get too excited about that. The man has a reputation for scandals."

"I know," Lilly said cheerfully. "Anyway, he promised he wouldn't say anything to Robert. And he's helping with the rest of my plan."

"What's the rest of your plan?"

"To get you to go to Robert. And you will go," Lilly said

sternly as Alyssum moved back a step.

"Things are getting complicated," Alyssum muttered. "It was just supposed to be one night, one kiss, with a man I would never know."

Lilly smiled. "Get dressed, Alyssum. You're about to have a second night, and a second kiss, with a man you know."

Alyssum chewed her bottom lip. "How do I see him without my mask?"

"I'll get it back. Now quickly." She looked to the clock. "We're running late."

Jackson looked at the clock in the corner of the room and tried not to grind his teeth in impatience. It was eleven o'clock. Where were they? He looked across the table to where Robert sat with a full drink in his hand.

"To almost capturing Scarlet." Jackson lifted his cup and clinked it with Robert's. He took a swig then lowered his cup and grouched that Robert wasn't drinking.

Get him drunk, Lilly's voice rang in his mind.

"Come on, Lambert. You're supposed to take a drink when there has been a toast."

Robert blew out his breath and took a drink. Thinking fast, Jackson dove forward and held the bottom of his cup up. Robert made a noise of distress but swallowed his drink before it splashed over him.

When Robert's cup was empty, he smacked it on the table and glared at Jackson. "What the hell was that?" he demanded, wiping some ale from his chin.

"You're moping," he stated. "Have another drink." He waved the barmaid over.

"Hello, my love," she purred.

"Two drinks, please," he ordered without looking at her.

"Okay, my love," she breathed then sauntered away.

Jackson groaned and dropped his head onto the table while Robert chuckled.

"Having fun?" he asked with a laugh.

"She won't leave me alone," Jackson muttered against the table. "I swear she's stalking me."

Robert laughed again.

"I only bedded her once. I managed to escape the last time we were here but now she won't leave me alone."

Robert cleared his throat to stop his laughing. "You must have made an impression."

"Hardly. I wasn't even trying," Jackson mumbled. He sat straight then leaned back in his chair as his stalker approached and placed the cups down.

"Anything else?" She stared down at Jackson with hungry eyes.

"Nope." Jackson shook his head. "This is all."

Jackson watched her leave. "No more barmaids," he spoke to himself.

Robert laughed. "You better be careful she may have poisoned your drink."

Jackson looked down at his cup. Staring at it with assessing eyes, he then reached over the table and swapped his cup with Robert's.

Robert burst into laughter.

"Well, drink it then," Jackson dared.

Robert raised the cup, saluted Jackson and downed the contents. Placing the cup on the table with a thud, he stared down at the mug with a frown then groaned. He looked up to Jackson. He groaned again and swayed on his seat.

"Lambert?" Jackson snapped, worried.

Robert fell forward and planted his face on to the table with a thud.

"Lambert!" Jackson stood and reached over. He paused as he saw Robert's shoulders shaking. With a sigh, he sat back down and watched as Robert raised his laughing face.

"I hope that hurt."

"Worth it." Robert laughed and rubbed his forehead.

Lilly and Alyssum peeked around the corner of the tavern. Black cloaks hiding their identity as they stared wide eyed at the tavern. Barmaids walked with jugs in their hands, their dresses low and revealing. Men groped and yelled drunkenly.

"Let's leave," Alyssum breathed, terrified.

"No way. Come on, let's get you upstairs and I'll send word for Jackson."

"Lilly," Alyssum's voice was filled with worry.

"Come on." Lilly grabbed Alyssum's hand and pulled her through the crowd. They caught a glimpse of Jackson and Robert across the room but managed to avoid detection as they hurried up the stairs to the rooms Lilly had secretly arranged.

Jackson knocked on the door to room five. It opened and a small hand reached out and pulled him in by his coat. He laughed as he was tugged into the dull candle-lit room and listened to the door shut behind him.

"Isn't this cozy," he said, as his gaze ran over the small room. A table and two chairs sat in one corner, a small writing desk against the wall, a privacy screen and then a single bed in the centre of the room. A door stood to his left, adjoining to the room next door. He looked behind him to the two women in black cloaks. "Love the look." He winked. "Miss Darrel." He nodded to one hooded figure. He turned to the other. "Miss Rosewood."

Lilly dragged her hood back with a gasp. "How did you know who was who?"

Jackson grinned then pointed his finger down to the floor. Lilly looked down and saw the hem of her white dress peaking out.

"You wear white," he answered.

"And you..." He looked to Alyssum. "Well, we all know what color dress you're wearing." He looked down to the scarlet hem peeking out from beneath her cloak.

She reached up with a black-gloved hand and pushed her hood back.

"Alyssum."

"My mask, Mr. West." She held out her hand.

Jackson reached into his pocket, brought out the mask and placed it in her waiting hand.

"He's not as drunk as you would like." He looked to Lilly. "But he's drank enough for her to knee him again if she wants." He turned his gaze back to Alyssum and saw a red blush heat her cheeks in the dark, shadowy room.

"He's waiting."

Alyssum turned to Lilly who stepped forward and gave her an encouraging hug. Jackson rolled his eyes.

"I expect you to keep your mouth shut," Alyssum snapped

at him and walked over to the bed. She untied her cloak and laid it down. She gave one last look back to Lilly before stepping through to the next room.

"She must know how to kiss," Jackson muttered while staring at the closed door.

He looked down as he felt Lilly shove his shoulder.

"That's my friend you're talking about."

"Would you rather I talk about you?" He arched a brow and grinned. And not just any grin, but the grin that he wore before he seduced and ruined a girl.

"I would love that. Perhaps you could take me in your arms and kiss me," she announced like an actress on stage, her hand at her heart, her eyes wide. "Then we could be married and live happily ever after."

"Quite the display," Jackson grumbled, a bit annoyed that she hadn't become star struck by his grin. Most girls did. Why wouldn't she, the little minx?

"Now you sit on your side of the room and I'll sit on mine." Lilly turned and marched over to the small writing table. She sat down on the wobbly wooden chair.

Jackson ignored her instructions and instead of sitting at the table on the other side of the room he walked over to the bed and slid onto it. He leaned back with a sigh and placed his arms behind his head.

Lilly grumbled at how comfortable he seemed.

"Would you care to join me?" he asked from the bed while he stared at the ceiling.

He smiled as he heard her harrumph.

As Robert sat at the table alone finishing his fourth ale, he watched as a blonde barmaid came over to him. He sighed as he remembered his past. Most of the women he'd been with had been blonde, a few red-head. But now all he wanted was midnight locks wrapped around his hands as he plundered deep-red lips.

The barmaid came and leaned her hip on the table. "There's a call for you coming from room four." She winked. "But if you want to join me in room ten you're most welcome."

Robert smiled with a soft laugh. The rooms upstairs were only used for one thing and sleeping wasn't it.

"A most generous offer I must decline," he told her. A month ago he would have taken both offers, but now, all he wanted was one woman—Scarlet.

She shrugged and her dress slipped farther off her shoulder, revealing more of her large breasts. Robert finished the rest of his ale.

"Will I be escorting you to room four?"

"I'll be declining that offer as well."

The blonde raised her eyebrows. "You're saying no to both offers?" she said surprised. She shrugged a flippant shoulder then walked away. He watched her walk up the stairs.

With a groan, he waved for another drink. *Hurry up, Jackson.*

As another drink was set before him he looked up in surprise as the blonde came back.

"The answer is still no," he told her gently but firmly.

"The girl's got a message for you."

Robert exhaled and shifted in his seat. It had been too long for him. He was a lusty man who liked to be bedded regularly.

"What is it?" he asked testy. Could these women not take no for an answer?

"She said to tell you her name is Scarlet."

His heart leaped. Was it really her? "Room four," he said dazedly.

"Yeah," she nodded then jumped back with a squeak as he jumped from his seat and ran up the stairs.

Robert didn't knock but opened the door and stumbled in. He threw the door shut behind him and stepped into the dark room. He frowned as the room looked empty. He shouldn't have drunken that fourth ale, he thought to himself as he swayed in dizziness. Movement by the window caught his attention. He squinted his eyes in the dark. No candles lit the room, only light from the window. "Scarlet?" He stepped farther into the room, making his way towards the window.

"You owe me a garter," a husky, shaky voiced reached him.

His breath caught as she stepped from the darkness. Her masked face was hidden in shadows but her scarlet gown was lit in silver light.

He moved forward, his steps eating up the distance between them. He saw the slight widening of her eyes behind her mask before he captured her face in his hands and smothered her gasp of surprise with his lips.

Alyssum felt drunk off his kiss. Her brain turned to mush as her body sparked with awareness and her stomach somersaulted with longing. He tunneled his hands into her unbound hair as his mouth moved roughly. She gasped as her back was suddenly pressed into the wall. She responded to his hunger by kissing him back wildly. Her tongue met his, her hands groped inside his coat, wanting to feel him.

His mouth left hers to kiss her cheek. His breath panted hotly against her skin as his mouth traveled over her jaw. "God, I've missed you," he whispered hoarsely. His lips moved to her neck. He licked then sucked.

131

She fisted her hands in his coat and her toes curled inside her shoes. She moaned then whimpered as he kissed her neck. Heat surged through her body, lighting her ablaze. She whimpered and arched into him, thrusting her breasts against his chest.

Robert took her hips in his hands. He nipped the cords of her neck. She arched to him, exposing her neck, wanting more. He breathed harshly against her skin as he took what was given.

He moaned deeply as she ran her hands up his chest. He raised his head from her neck and captured her mouth with his. He pinned her flush against the wall and rubbed his hard body against the softness of hers.

As she took lead of the kiss, stroking his tongue, nipping his lips with her teeth, he ground his throbbing shaft against her. She released his mouth with a gasp and their gazes met in the dark.

Their harsh breathing mingled while their gazes stayed locked.

Alyssum felt her heart pounding. Her hands curled into his coat at his shoulders. She was with Robert. A smile curved her lips.

Her mouth captured his and they kissed slowly this time. She moaned in pleasure and sank back against the wall. She tilted her head for his slow, plundering kiss.

"Robert," she gasped as she clutched him to her.

Robert froze. Her hands pulled on his coat, urging him to keep going but he raised his head, staring down at her. "You know who I am." His voice was rough, like it had been on the balcony. His expression turned hard then he was reaching for her mask.

She went wild in his arms as his fingers touched her mask at her temples. She shoved him, pushed him and even bit him.

"Ow!" Robert looked at his hand that she had bitten. "Who are you?" he demanded. "Why is it so bad for me to know who you are?" He watched her panting against the wall, slightly slinking away. He took a step towards her and she ducked around him. He grabbed her skirt and yanked her back to him. Her back hit his chest.

"Why don't you want me to know?" he breathed in her ear. "Are you married?" he asked, fearful.

"No," she whispered.

Robert breathed a sigh of relief as he rested his forehead against her temple. "This is our secret," he whispered. He then reached for the tie at the back of her hair.

He pulled the tie and she struggled in his arms with a new strength. He grunted as she kicked his shin. The mask slipped from her face and fluttered to the floor. He followed the mask with his gaze and watched as it landed on the floor.

Alyssum stared, gaping at her mask on the floor at her feet. It was dark in the room, but all he had to do was drag her to the window to find out her identity.

She suddenly heard Harry's voice in her head, *Lesson number two in protecting your virtue.*

She turned quickly in Robert's arms. His gaze was on the floor but as she turned he moved to look up. Her heart skipped a beat as they stared at one another. Robert was looking at her, but he couldn't see her.

Robert squinted in the dark again. He grabbed Scarlet's arm, about to drag her to the light at the window. He paused as he saw her face coming closer to his.

Alyssum saw stars and pain erupted in her head. She

gasped and gripped her forehead. Harry hadn't told her it would hurt so much.

Robert swayed on his feet after her forehead struck his. While he was dazed, Scarlet swooped up her mask from the floor and ran for the adjoining door.

Lilly stood from the chair across the room as Alyssum flew in and locked the door behind her.

Already seeing her urgency, Lilly grabbed her cloak and drew it on.

"What did you do to him this time?" Jackson asked as he sat up on the bed.

Alyssum swayed on her feet as she held her forehead.

"You head clocked him?" Jackson asked impressed.

"Harry taught me," she told him as she grabbed her cloak from the bed.

"I bet he also taught you knee to man's bollocks?" he asked while watching her put on her cloak and draw the hood up.

"Yes," she replied.

All gazes swung to the adjoining door as Robert hammered his fist on it. "Open the door, Scarlet," he shouted.

"He sounds mad," Lilly whispered.

"You think?" Jackson arched a brow.

When Robert slammed into the door, making it rattle, Alyssum grabbed Lilly's wrist and pulled her from the room. Jackson followed after them.

Chapter Nine

Alyssum woke with a splitting headache. Her eyes drifted closed as she remembered Robert's embrace, the way he had moved against her. She wanted more, much more.

Last night had been different from the night they had first kissed. That night on the balcony she had kissed a masked stranger, but last night she had kissed Robert and loved it.

Alyssum looked up as a light knock came to her door. "Come in," she called as she slid from the bed.

Meg walked in. She paused as her gaze landed on Alyssum's forehead. "My lady, what happened?" she gaped as she stared at the yellow bruise on Alyssum's forehead.

"Oh, I walked into a cupboard in the kitchen."

Meg nodded. "Which gown would you like to wear to Lord Avery's dinner party?"

"Oh," Alyssum breathed. She had forgotten about Lord Avery's. Hopefully her headache would be gone before nightfall. "Um, the blue one with the gold embroidery."

"Yes, miss." Meg moved around the room as Alyssum walked to the basin and cleaned her face with cold water. She sighed as the cold water touched her bruised forehead. She touched the bruise and winced. "Damn it," she muttered under her breath.

Violet looked up from her spot in the garden, gasped and

stood.

"What happened to you?" she asked Alyssum as she stared at the ugly yellow bruise.

"That's what we need to figure out." Alyssum moved aside her yellow skirt and sat down on the blanket that rested over the grass.

Violet sat down beside her. "What did you do, Alyssum?" she looked at her sister with worry.

"I saw Robert."

Violet nodded for her to continue.

"As Scarlet," she finished.

Violet's mouth shaped into an O. She then nodded one more time slowly. "Does he know?"

"No." Alyssum shook her head then winced and touched her bruise.

"Lesson two," Violet muttered.

"Yes," Alyssum replied while still holding her head.

"He's lucky you didn't use lesson five."

Alyssum chuckled.

"All right. You bumped your head," Violet said casually.

"I told Meg I knocked into a cupboard in the kitchen."

Violet nodded. "You were getting a midnight snack," she said.

Alyssum smiled. "You're a genius."

Violet smiled and shrugged a careless shoulder.

Robert rolled over with a groan. He shouted as he was suddenly weightless and then thumped to the floor. He dragged himself up and looked at his surroundings. He nodded, recognizing his bedroom in his London townhouse.

Standing on wobbly legs, he stumbled over the bottle of port he had drunk last night. After losing Scarlet for the third time, he had left Jackson at the tavern and swallowed his sorrows in a bottle. He couldn't believe it. He had had her. In his sight, in his arms and she had gotten away, again. He had been so close. He had removed her mask. If only there had been a candle lit in the room, then he would know right now who she was. He could still remember the feel of her. Soft, luscious curves. Her bottom lip much fuller than her upper lip. Her faintly rose-scented skin. Long, wavy tresses, softer than her skin.

With a grumble, he reached the dresser and poured water into the basin. He splashed his face and gasped against the cold. He splashed his face over and over, clearing his muddled brain.

He turned his head towards the door as his valet walked in. Thomas crinkled his nose at Robert's disorderly state. Still wearing his clothes from last night, he was a wrinkled mess.

"A bath first," Robert croaked then cleared his throat.

Thomas nodded. "Lord Avery's dinner party tonight," he reminded Robert before leaving the room.

Robert groaned loudly. He had forgotten completely about tonight's event.

Lord Avery. A rich man. A brilliant man. A complete nodcock. He was well known in society for his snobbish manner and famous art gallery that he loved to boast about. Lord Avery held a dinner party every year to show off a new piece of art in his large collection. And he was also a well-known admirer of

137

Lady Alyssum Rosewood.

"Don't leave me alone with the man," Alyssum whispered to Violet as they stood in the line to enter Lord Avery's house. "Not for one second," she whispered as she stared at the largely built man. He looked like a boxer with his meaty hands and round face.

Violet smiled at her sister. "Calm down," she whispered back as the line drew them closer to Lord Avery. "I'll protect you." She giggled.

Alyssum took a deep breath before stepping before Lord Avery.

His hand caught hers and he placed a wet kiss to the back of her hand. Alyssum tried not to cringe at her ruined glove.

"You look lovely, Lady Rosewood." His dark eyes ran over her, taking in her deep blue dress. His eyes paused and stayed on her bodice.

Alyssum tugged her hand but he was too busy ogling her breasts to release her.

"Lord Avery," a man's loud, happy voice broke Avery's gaze. Alyssum took her hand back but her unease didn't settle as she looked up to her rescuer.

Robert grinned down at Alyssum. Her stomach did that irritating flip and desire rushed through her veins as last night's events came crashing down on her. Pinned between his body and the wall, his mouth on her while he rubbed his hard body against hers. She swallowed audibly. "Viscount Lambert." She curtsied. She took a quick glimpse behind Robert and found Violet smiling at her. She would speak to her later, for now she had to get through this.

"Lady Alyssum, you look ravishing." Robert said.

Alyssum felt her body responding, heat blooming between

her thighs. She ached.

"Excuse me," she said a little too loudly. She curtseyed fast then walked away from Robert and Avery.

Walking through the crowded parlor, Alyssum kept her gaze straight ahead and not back towards the line where Robert stood.

"Alyssum!"

She gasped as someone caught her arm. She then relaxed as she saw Lilly's smiling face.

"Jumpy tonight, are we?"

"You could say that," Alyssum muttered.

"Nice haircut." Lilly inspected Alyssum's newly cut fringe. Wisps of her black hair were swept over her forehead.

"I had to hide the bruise," Alyssum whispered then, with a quick look around to find no gazes on them, she swept aside the fringe Meg had cut for her.

"Smart." Lilly nodded. "And ouch."

Alyssum smoothed her fringe back in place. "It was Violet's idea. We applied so much powder I looked like a clown, then Violet came up with the idea of a fringe."

"He'll never see it."

"If anyone asks, I knocked into a kitchen cupboard."

"Done." Lilly nodded once.

"You look wonderful by the way."

Lilly's smile brightened and caught a few passing gentlemen's gazes. "Thank you." Lilly looked down to her light pink dress. "I finally got Mother to let me wear something other than white."

"Well, it looks lovely."

"Quite. You should wear the color more often, Miss Darrel,"

139

Jackson said as he stepped up beside the girls.

They both shifted nervous gazes at him.

"Though I prefer to see you in scarlet." He winked.

Lilly gasped and kicked his shin. Jackson hid his cringe and laughed instead.

Lilly's cheeks flushed red at her actions but Violet saved her from having to apologize as she stepped into the circle.

"Lady Violet." Jackson bowed to her. "I dare hope you won't kick me."

Violet looked to Lilly and Alyssum in confusion. "No." She shook her head to Jackson.

"I'm glad."

The back of Alyssum's neck tingled. Her skin sizzled as she felt someone's gaze on her.

"Ladies," Robert voice spoke directly behind her. She drew her back straighter, her chin notching higher. Lilly noticed and gave a small shake of her head in disapproval.

Alyssum turned and stepped aside, giving Robert entry into the circle.

Their gazes caught and held as he moved in. He then turned to Jackson. "Are you behaving?"

Jackson grinned in reply and looked down at Lilly, who kept her gaze averted.

"Miss Darrel," a stern voice broke the circle.

They all saw Lilly exhale miserably. She then turned to her stern chaperon.

"Coming, Miss Rickton." Lilly turned back to the group and gave a small curtsey. She then turned on her heel and followed Miss Rickton back to her parents.

"Lady Violet, would you like to join me in viewing Lord

Avery's new piece of art?" Jackson offered her his elbow.

Violet smiled at Alyssum as she took Jackson's offered arm and answered, "I would love to." Jackson and Violet both smiled knowingly at Alyssum then turned and left her and Robert alone.

Robert watched Jackson and Violet walk through the bustling crowd before turning to face Alyssum. "Pity there's no dancing tonight. You owe me a dance."

"I do not," she replied, while ignoring how her body wanted to sway into his and melt.

"You do. I know you were about to accept my offer of a dance before Miss Darrel interrupted us. It seems she does that a lot."

"She has good timing."

Robert chuckled. "You wound me."

"You exaggerate."

Robert didn't chuckle this time but laughed loudly. People standing nearby looked at them.

"Stop it," Alyssum said in a hushed tone as she looked at the people around her.

"Ah, wouldn't want society to know that we're happy."

"It's not that."

"Then what?" He arched a brow and waited.

"People are watching."

"You don't like to be seen, do you?" he asked as he took a small step forward.

Alyssum was completely aware of his approach. She took a small step back. "I prefer if people kept to their own business and not get involved in mine."

"Well said." Robert nodded with a smile.

Alyssum twitched her lips and looked away before she found herself stepping towards him and seeing if he still smelled the same, warm, male and arousing.

"Is that Miss Gilbert talking to Harry?" Alyssum asked anxiously as she saw a young blonde speaking to Harry.

Robert followed Alyssum's gaze quickly then muttered a curse that made Alyssum's eyes widen.

"That's her," Robert ground out between clenched teeth. Miss Mariah Gilbert was one of many people in society who loved to speak ill of Harry's scar. Robert and Alyssum watched as closely as they could through the crowd in the parlor. They watched as Harry stared not at Miss Gilbert but straight ahead. They noticed his jaw tick as she spoke.

"Excuse me."

"Pardon me." They both paused as they had spoken instantaneously. Robert stepped aside and waved her forward. Alyssum began crossing the parlor to make her way towards her brother. Robert walked right behind her.

"So good to see you here," Alyssum's voice dripped with sweetness as she spoke to Mariah and stood by her brother. "And how lovely you look tonight." Alyssum's gaze ran down Mariah's yellow dress.

Robert stood on the other side of Harry. His icy gaze staring at Mariah.

"Thank you." Mariah beamed at Alyssum's complement and she ran her hands over the dress.

"I believe I had the same gown once." Alyssum titled her head, looking at the gown. "But that must have been years ago. I stay with the latest fashions. Very daring of you to wear such an outdated gown." She smiled brightly, sweetly.

Mariah froze as she realized she had just been insulted. Her mouth moved to bite out a retort.

"Excuse us will you, Miss Gilbert." Alyssum slid her arm around Harry's "I would like my dear brother to take me to speak to the Duke of Linkinshire. He has such high-standing friends." She pulled Harry away from a gaping Miss Gilbert.

"I hate it when you do that," Harry muttered as they walked away.

"I love it when she does that," Robert spoke as he walked beside Alyssum.

Alyssum found herself smiling as she held Harry's arm and he led them over to Duke, who was swamped with eligible ladies and their mothers.

"Poor man." Robert shuddered at the young, innocent misses.

"That'll be you one day," Harry replied.

"You too." Robert retorted. They both had titles that needed heirs.

Duke caught sight of Harry and Robert approaching. They smiled at him as they noticed his distress.

"Excuse me, ladies." He bowed respectfully and pulled himself out of the group. He sighed as he reached Harry and Robert. He nodded down to Alyssum. "Lady Alyssum."

"Duke." She smiled.

Robert looked down at her in surprise. "You call him Duke but you won't call me by my first name?"

Alyssum ignored him. "How is your night faring, Duke?"

Duke smiled as he noticed Alyssum ignoring Robert. "Demanding," he replied to her question.

"They won't leave you alone until you marry and produce an heir." She shook her head sympathetically.

"Well, if you're offering?" He grinned. Even at thirty, Duke's grin was young and roguish, making her grin back.

"Watch it," Harry warned.

Duke smiled and nodded his head to Harry, obviously understanding the protectiveness between Harry and his sisters.

"Excuse me," Robert grumbled then turned and left. Harry watched him leave with a frown.

When he turned his gaze back to Duke, Duke arched a brow and Harry nodded.

"Excuse me, Alyssum." Duke bowed his head then left and followed after Robert.

"You too?" Alyssum looked up to Harry, who smiled.

"I'll see you at dinner." He patted her hand then disentangled his arm from hers.

Alyssum watched as Harry and Duke walked towards Robert who stood beside a servant and took a drink from the tray.

As Robert took the brandy from the tray, he tried to dull out his sudden anger at seeing Alyssum flirting with Duke. He had never seen her like that, smiling, grinning at another man. He now wondered how many men she had flirted with when he never even thought about Alyssum with men. She had always just been Alyssum to him. Simple, infuriating, beautiful Alyssum.

"Robert, are you all right?" Harry asked as he and Duke appeared beside him.

"I'm fine." He took a sip of his drink. "Boring night, is it not?"

"I've found it quite eventful," Duke replied.

"Robert, Lisa Knight is here tonight," Harry informed him.

"Great. Just what I needed." He looked over to the doorway in time to see Alyssum leaving the room, probably on her way to view Lord Avery's art collection. He drank the rest of the brandy in one gulp and set the empty glass on the table. "Excuse me," he muttered and stalked away.

Robert's boots thudded over the floor as he made his way to the cause of his anger. Alyssum stood smiling beside Violet and Jackson in Avery's gallery. Jackson's gaze caught his as he approached and his friend frowned, obviously noticing the anger in Robert's gaze. He stepped forward, leaving the girls to stand before Robert.

"What are you doing?" he muttered, but Robert ignored him, stepped around him and stood before Alyssum.

"Enjoying yourself?" he asked.

Alyssum's smile slipped as she looked up at Robert. "It's a nice evening, yes."

Violet and Jackson both watched them carefully.

"Enjoy speaking with Duke?"

A crease furrowed Alyssum's brow as she answered. "Yes."

"It seemed you did."

"What are you getting at?" She took an angry step forward, tilting her head back to look at him.

"Nothing. You just seemed quite a natural at flirting with Duke."

Jackson groaned behind him, while Violet's eyes widened as she watched intently.

"Excuse me?" Alyssum whispered with wrath and took another step forward. "I was doing what?"

"Flirting." He nodded with a tight smile. "You did it quite well. Looking to become a duchess?"

"Oh." Alyssum breathed deeply and shook her head. "You're one to talk. How many women have you flirted with?"

"Lost count." Robert shrugged.

"How many women have you snuck out onto the terrace with during dinners, luncheons, balls?"

"Why do you ask?" He took a step forward, almost brushing her chest with his. "Would you like to join me on the terrace?" he spoke quietly to her.

"Oh, no," Violet whispered and looked around to check that no one else was in gallery.

Alyssum, no longer able to speak in her rage, raised her foot and brought it down hard on Robert's boot. She smiled as Robert cringed and groaned.

"Anything else you would like to say?" she demanded.

"He's done." Jackson stepped in, grabbed Robert's arm and dragged him out of the gallery and back into the parlor.

"What do you think you're doing?" Jackson demanded as they walked through the parlor. "You want Harry to kick your ass?"

Robert grumbled then stopped limping.

"Well?" Jackson demanded. "What the hell happened back there?"

"I didn't like seeing her flirting with Duke," Robert snapped.

Jackson ran his gaze over the crowd and paused on a young miss with black hair. "There's Lisa Knight."

Robert looked through the crowd then stared at the smiling Miss Knight. She was completely unaware that she was on a list that rested inside Robert's coat.

"Are you going to go talk to her?"

Robert shook his head slowly. "Not tonight," he muttered and looked away.

"You do realize that could be Scarlet?"

Before Robert could reply, a servant stepped into the room. "Dinner is served," he announced.

They filed into the dining room and took their seats. Robert's gaze was on Alyssum as she sat on the opposite side of the table, farther up.

He was staring at her again. Alyssum shifted in her seat and kept her gaze fixed on Lord Avery who was speaking. Her neck tingled with complete awareness of Robert's gaze. She couldn't believe the anger he'd displayed in the gallery. She had just been talking to Duke, and he had dared to call her a flirt.

Taking deep breaths, she concentrated on Lord Avery who seemed very pleased to have her undivided attention. But even though her eyes were on him, her mind was on Robert. Her heart began beating faster as she remembered their rendezvous at the tavern. She could see his eyes as he stared down at her with passion, feel his body molding to hers as his hands clutched her to him. It had been so different. They had reunited in a fiery passion, wanting each other so desperately over the week that they had been separated. She didn't know how much longer she could be around Robert as just Alyssum and not give herself away somehow. She found herself wanting to kiss him every time he stood near her. Even when he was angering her.

After dinner, the ladies left the room and returned to the parlor while the men stayed to have their port.

"You couldn't keep your eyes off her," a gentleman laughed as he spoke to Avery.

Harry looked over and listened to the conversation.

"Lady Alyssum *is* mesmerizing," Avery replied, which caught Harry and Robert's attention.

"Excuse me, gentlemen." Harry stood and walked towards the parlor. He knew to leave before Avery started fishing around at marrying Alyssum.

He made his way straight to his sisters and mother. "Fifteen more minutes and we're leaving," he whispered.

"Thank God," Alyssum replied quietly. Violet laughed when their mother huffed.

"Well, I'm enjoying myself," she told her children.

"That's because you don't have Avery drooling down your chest," Harry said, which caused Alyssum and Violet to laugh and Caroline to huff louder.

Harry looked over as the other men entered the parlor. He spotted Jackson, Robert and Duke. "Excuse me." He nodded his head to his family and made his way across the room and out onto the terrace.

"What's going on?" he asked the men as they all stood out on the terrace.

"It's not Lisa Knight," Robert announced.

"And how do you know that?" Harry crossed his arms.

"I've had Scarlet up against me aplenty. I know her body and Lisa doesn't have the same curves."

"He's trying to say her breasts are too small."

"Thank you, Jackson," Robert said and Jackson nodded.

"So it's Katherine Jenkins. Congratulations," Harry said.

"There is still someone on that list," Duke spoke cautiously.

Harry glared. Duke shrugged and leaned back on the railing, pulling a cigar out of his coat pocket. "Is anyone going to say it?" he asked as he lit the cigar and took a long draw.

"Alyssum Rosewood," Jackson said with a grin.

"You want another black eye?" Harry asked.

Jackson sighed. "It just healed," he muttered.

"Alyssum is beautiful," Duke said. He then held his hands out as Harry and Robert glared.

"It's a possibility you should at least check," he mumbled around his cigar.

"I'm with Duke, and I speak for Tucker as well," Jackson said.

"Where is Tucker?" Harry asked.

"His father," Duke answered and they all murmured in understanding.

"Anyone notice Alyssum's new haircut?" Jackson muttered and Harry sighed for patience.

"Scarlet," Harry snapped, "is not Alyssum."

"We'll see," Jackson replied.

"What about her new haircut?" Robert asked, confused.

"It looks nice," Duke said.

"It's covering her forehead," Jackson said exasperated. "Doesn't anyone see that? Robert, you told us when Alyssum saw you again she head clocked you. I think that would cause a bruise." He stared at them like they were idiots then frowned as they all stared at him strangely. "What?"

"You said when Alyssum saw him again," Duke answered.

"Did I? Huh. That's just because I think it's her." He shrugged his shoulder then jumped back as Harry came for him.

"Easy." Duke grabbed Harry before he reached Jackson. "We're not in the tavern." He shoved him back.

"When we leave this house..." Harry warned Jackson.

"I'm shaking," Jackson mocked, causing Harry to growl.

"Harry, when did Alyssum cut her hair?" Robert asked dazedly.

"I don't know, I only just noticed it when Jackson mentioned it."

Robert furrowed his brow.

"I'm heading home," Harry muttered then turned and walked back inside the parlor.

"He's not going to consider it, is he?" Duke muttered.

"There's nothing to consider. Alyssum isn't Scarlet," Robert snapped angrily and walked back into the parlor as well.

On the carriage ride back home, Alyssum noticed Harry looking at her strangely. When they arrived back home and entered the foyer she noticed him frowning in thought. Worried he was about to ask her more questions or ask about her new haircut, she excused herself to her bedroom and walked up the stairs quickly.

After entering her bedroom, she sighed but then jumped as a knock came to her door. Taking a deep breath, she turned and opened it. She kept her face serene as she saw Harry standing outside the door.

"Can I speak to you?" he asked, his tone low and serious.

She nodded jerkily and opened the door wide. He walked in then looked around her room.

"What would you like to speak to me about?"

Harry took a deep breath before saying, "Lady Brook's masquerade." Alyssum made herself smile. "I must have missed quite a night." She shook her head. "Everyone wants to know everything about that night."

"No." Harry stepped forward. "We want to know who the woman in scarlet was."

Alyssum shrugged while her heart raced and her palms grew damp. "I don't think I got to see her."

"The blue dress you wore that night, may I see it?"

Alyssum frowned but nodded. "Of course." She walked around him and opened her wardrobe. She reached in, pushed some dresses aside then pulled out a blue silk dress.

She held it up to him.

"It's lovely." He nodded.

"It's a shame I didn't get to wear it for longer."

"What about the blue mask?"

"It's somewhere in here." She pointed into her full wardrobe. She watched as Harry rubbed his forehead with his palm.

"Are you all right, Harry?" she asked, worried about him. He was acting strangely.

"I like your new haircut," he told her.

She smiled and touched her strategically placed fringe. "Thank you."

"Did Meg do it?" he asked as he stepped towards her and moved to touch her hair.

"Yes," she replied and stepped back. "It's been a long night, Harry. I would like some sleep."

Harry nodded and took a step back. "Good night."

"Good night."

She closed the door with a deep sigh after Harry left. After putting the blue dress back in the wardrobe, she pulled her own gown off and laid it over the chair in front of her dressing table.

Sitting on her bed in her undergarments, Alyssum frowned with worry. Harry was suspicious. She feared he would soon find out the truth that she was Scarlet.

Chapter Ten

*He ran his smooth, soft lips over the sensitive skin at her neck. Her whole body shivered as his tongue licked the rim of her ear. Alyssum felt her body growing hotter by the second as Robert's warm, naked body lowered over hers, pinning her to the mattress. She gasped as they touched skin to skin. He nudged her legs apart with his as he nibbled at her ear and smoothed his hands over her breasts. She arched and moaned into his touch. He held her breasts in his palms as he nudged his cock against her quivering entrance. She ached with need for him. Running her hands down his hard, muscled back, she moaned at the feel of him then gripped his buttocks in her greedy hands. Robert bit her ear then thrust his hips forward, plunging himself deep inside her wet, giving body. Alyssum groaned...*then cried out at the sudden pain she felt.

Sitting up in her bed, Alyssum looked around and found Violet standing beside her bed. The morning sun shone in through the open curtains. "What are you doing in here?" she demanded. "Did you pinch me?" Alyssum looked down to where her arm hurt.

"You wouldn't wake up," Violet answered. She then tilted her head and stared at Alyssum. "You look a fright."

Alyssum sighed and pushed her fringe out of her eyes. Violet cringed at seeing the yellow bruise. "It's fading," she said as she inspected it. "But it still looks terrible. How hard did you crack him?"

"Hard enough," Alyssum muttered and stood from the bed.

"How's your finger?" Violet looked to her bandaged index finger.

"With the bruise giving me a constant headache I don't really notice it."

Violet nodded with a smile. "You're running late."

"How do you mean?" Alyssum turned as she stood before the water pitcher and basin, ready to wash her face.

"You slept through breakfast and we have a luncheon to attend at the Darrel's."

Alyssum nodded, remembering.

"Alyssum, why was Robert so angry with you last night?"

Alyssum was silent for a moment before answering. "I don't know. Now please leave, I've got to get ready."

"You have fifteen minutes," Violet told her as she walked towards the door, already dressed and ready to go.

"All right. Send Meg up."

"I will." Violet shut the bedroom door behind her.

Walking through the Darrel's townhouse, Alyssum couldn't help but admire the richly furnished rooms. Alyssum looked at the white tables set out as she stepped onto the sunny terrace. She looked through the small gathering and smiled when she found Lilly surrounded by admirers while a stern-faced Rickton watched closely.

"I'm going to go talk to Lilly," Alyssum told Violet. "Come with me."

Violet shook her head quickly when she saw how many men were surrounding Lilly. "I'll stay here."

Alyssum smiled in understanding then left her side to go to

Lilly.

Lilly spotted her walking towards her and smiled. "Excuse me." She nudged her way through her admirers and reached Alyssum halfway across the terrace.

"What do you think?" Lilly looked around.

"You did a wonderful job."

"Thank you." Lilly beamed. "My parents are still waiting for some disaster to happen."

At that moment, Lilly's mother reached their side and whispered furiously to her daughter, "You invited *him*." Lilly took after her mother in hair color, eye color and beauty. They were both short, petite woman.

Both Lilly and Alyssum looked over to the doorway to the terrace and saw Robert step out onto the terrace. Alyssum felt her lips tugging into a smile as she saw his cravat was askew. Her body also warmed as she remembered her dream.

"He will behave," Lilly told her mother. "Plus, he is held very high in society."

"He is only regarded highly in society because of his scandals."

"He has never harmed anyone. His scandals are riding his curricle too fast or...diving into the Thames half-naked."

Lilly's mother gasped in mortification.

"And at one time he climbed a very large tree to save a cat," Lilly continued.

"Enough. Just have the servants keep close eyes on him."

"I will." Lilly smiled then gave her mother a kiss on the cheek.

"Good to see you, dear." Lilly's mother smiled at Alyssum.

"You too, Mrs. Darrel."

Mrs. Darrel bustled around the terrace, making sure everything was in order.

"I invited him just for you," Lilly whispered.

"Hush," Alyssum whispered back but watched as Robert walked around the tables and stood with Harry, Tucker and Duke.

"I can't believe the Duke of Linkinshire came," Lilly said with excitement. "I thought he would reject the invite."

"Well, now it's a definite that today will be a great success for you."

"It will." Lilly smiled and relaxed.

Alyssum smiled back, but she found her gaze wandering back to Robert speaking to Tucker.

"You didn't invite Mr. West?" Alyssum asked cautiously.

Lilly smile dropped into an annoyed frown. "He rejected the invite," she grumbled.

"Well, that's no matter, you have a duke here."

"Precisely." Lilly's smile returned as she looked over the terrace and watched her guests enjoy themselves.

"Can't you just try what your father asks?" Robert asked.

Tucker gaped. "Did you hear what he wants me to do?"

"Behave yourself?"

Tucker grumbled. "He wants me to turn into a pompous, plain gentleman."

"Just stay out of trouble for a while and your father will loosen the purse strings."

"Maybe," Tucker grouched and took a sip of the punch he was holding.

"Where did you get that?" Robert asked.

"Over there." He pointed back to the entrance of the terrace where a table stood with drinks.

"Ah." Robert nodded to Tucker then made his way over to the table.

He nodded to the servant who stood behind the table, looked down to the drinks and stifled a sigh that there wasn't anything stronger than punch. He jumped slightly as he felt someone grab his hand and pull him. When he looked up he found it was Alyssum tugging him back inside the house. She pulled him to a stop behind the doors inside the townhouse. Robert's heart was already beating faster, but it pounded when her hands reached up and unraveled his cravat. He swallowed visibly as he found himself wanting her to take off more than his cravat.

"You'll never do this right, will you?" she muttered as she straightened it to perfection.

"Not when I have you," he found himself saying. He smiled as he saw her smiling.

When she looked up, he exhaled slowly, calming his heart's reaction to the sight of her.

"Then get your valet to do it for you."

Robert shook his head with a cringe. "There's something about a grown man dressing me that doesn't sit well with me." He smiled brightly as Alyssum laughed.

"Much better." Alyssum surveyed her work. "Now you look like a gentleman and not a rake."

"Pity." He grinned.

"If you hadn't noticed," Alyssum spoke quietly, "this was my way of apologizing for stomping on your foot last night."

Robert nodded with a grin. "Apology accepted." He tilted his head. "So what am I going to have to do for you to accept my apology for being rude?"

"So you did notice you were being rude?" She placed her hands on her hips.

Robert laughed softly. "I noticed."

"Well, then you can just apologize with your words."

"I would much rather do it with my hands like you did." The look in her eyes made his temperature rise.

"N-no, you don't have to do that," she stuttered nervously.

Robert's grin widened as he noticed her stutter. He found himself stepping closer to her. The chatter of the people outside was drowned out by the sight of Alyssum's wide green eyes staring up at him. Mesmerized, he reached his hand out and brushed her fringe aside, moving her hair away from her gorgeous green eyes. He stilled his hand as she flinched. With a quick flick of his fingers, he swept her fringe aside and revealed a bruise on her forehead. He snapped out of his dazed trance as he saw the bruise.

"What happened?" he demanded in concern.

Alyssum smacked his hand away and pushed her fringe back in place. "I knocked it on a cupboard in the kitchen. It was clumsy of me and I would appreciate it if you didn't tell anyone."

"You knocked it on a cupboard?" he repeated as his hand moved to see the bruise again.

"Yes." She smacked his raised hand aside. "Now excuse me." She stepped around the door, left the shadowed area and walked out onto the terrace.

Robert stared after her until he lost her in the crowd. His hand rose to his own forehead.

He had iced his bruise quickly and had been lucky that it had faded the next morning. Holding the spot Scarlet had hit, he thought of Alyssum's bruise and found it was in the right spot. Their bruises matched. Not possible. She couldn't be...could she? She would never kiss him or sneak into a tavern to see him. Would she? It was mad, but a part him craved it to be real. He was stunned by how much he yearned for it to be true. But it couldn't be. He had seen it with his own eyes. Scarlet had come to the theatre. She had stood down in the pit while Alyssum had been sitting in her family's box.

Shaking his head clear, he stepped around the door and walked back outside. He grabbed a drink as he passed the table and walked back to the edge of the terrace where Harry and Tucker stood.

"Is Duke already mingling?" Robert asked and leaned back on the railing like Tucker and Harry were doing.

"Yep," Tucker answered, his eyes watching the crowd. "Look at them," he muttered as he watched the laughing crowd. "Scavengers."

Harry laughed and shook his head.

While Harry and Tucker talked, Robert's eyes wandered over the gathering until he saw Alyssum.

It was as he stared at her that he knew he wanted her. It struck his heart like a punch. Watching her smile and laugh softly, his whole body came alive. He wanted her. He always had, always would.

"If everyone would take their seats," Lilly called out and everyone moved for their assigned seats.

As the men pushed off the railing and made their way to the tables, Lilly passed them and smiled at Harry. Robert frowned as he noticed the look. "Are you interested in her?" he asked while nodding back to Lilly.

Harry laughed. "I'm not getting in the way of one of my friends."

"What do you mean?"

"You haven't seen it?" Harry arched a brow.

"Who?" Robert asked while looking to Tucker then Duke sitting over at the other table.

Harry laughed and sat in his chair while Robert grumbled and made his way over to the next table where he was assigned. He stepped up to his assigned seat and looked to see who was beside him. "Violet." He smiled happily.

"Hello, Robert." She smiled back.

"You look lovely." He looked at her turquoise dress.

"Thank you. You look well."

"Thank you." He bowed his head. As someone stepped up on the other side of him, he turned his gaze to see who it was. He felt the pleasure down to his toes as he stared at Alyssum. She gave him a guarded look but smiled at Violet.

"I don't get a smile?" he asked in mock hurt.

Alyssum twitched her lips at him then looked over to Lilly's table. Lilly was already watching her and when their gazes caught she gave Alyssum a wink. Alyssum shook her head at her.

Lunch went quickly. Robert spoke to Violet while Alyssum kept to herself. Afterwards most people stood and moved around the terrace. Robert excused himself and walked over to Harry and Tucker.

"He did it on purpose," Violet said as she watched Alyssum watching Robert.

"Pardon?" Alyssum turned her attention to Violet.

"He only spoke to me to annoy you."

"Oh, I don't mind." Alyssum looked over the crowed and spotted Lilly. She smiled then stood from her chair and walked over to her friend.

"You are in so much trouble," she muttered when she stood beside Lilly.

"Did you enjoy lunch?" Lilly asked with a sweet, innocent smile.

Alyssum shook her head at her. Lilly laughed then gasped as she caught sight of something behind Alyssum. "How dare he?" she whispered in anger.

Alyssum turned and found Jackson standing with Harry, Robert and Tucker.

"He declined the invite."

"He does this sometimes," Alyssum said.

"He's not getting away with this." Lilly marched over towards Jackson.

Alyssum laughed softly as she saw Lilly speaking quickly with an angry flush in her cheeks. Turning her gaze from the argument she walked to the edge of the terrace. With a look around she made her way to the stairs and walked down. The further she walked the quieter it became. She walked around the large hedge that blocked the party from her sight and found a beautiful white gazebo standing tall. She smiled and walked towards it.

Robert stepped around the hedge and stopped. Alyssum stood in the gazebo with her back facing him. He stared at the back of her elegant neck. Her black curls were pinned up, not a curl out of place. He remembered a time when she had always worn it out. Her nanny had run around the house trying to catch her and pin her hair up like a proper lady.

With a smile on his lips, he looked at the lady she had become. Beautiful, elegant, graceful, nothing like the girl he had once known and loved. But still loved. After all this time, he was still in love with Alyssum. The girl he had fallen in love with at eighteen.

Ten years ago

After the funeral of the former Viscount Lambert, Robert lounged on the chaise lounge in his father's precious office. With his boot-clad feet up on the lounge and a bottle of brandy in his hand, Robert was completely relaxed and happy for the first time in this house.

A scuffle outside the door had him turning his head.

"Sod off!"

Robert smiled as he heard Alyssum's voice cursing on the other side off the door. There was a grunt then a yelp and then the door swung open. Herbert, his father's butler, hopped on one foot as he held the other. Alyssum ran into the room and slammed the door shut.

"He wouldn't let me in," Alyssum said as she pointed her thumb behind her at the door. Still garbed in a black gown from the funeral, Alyssum shoved Robert's feet off the chaise and sat down.

"What are you doing?" She looked at the crystal bottle in his hand.

"Want some?" He offered her the bottle.

Alyssum cringed and shook her head. Robert took a drink from the bottle.

"Are you okay?" she asked softly.

Robert groaned. "People need to stop asking me that."

"Sorry." Alyssum placed a loose curl behind her ear.

"Does your father know you're here?"

Alyssum shrugged, which caused Robert to smile. "Guess not," he said and took a drink.

"Robert, why are you drinking?"

"I'm celebrating. My father's dead." He raised the bottle then took a large swallow before lowering it with a cringe.

Alyssum reached out and took the bottle from his hand. Too drunk to care, Robert just smiled.

Alyssum placed the bottle on the floor. "Why don't we go for a walk? It's still light outside."

Robert turned his head behind him to the window. The sky was pink as the afternoon sun slowly faded. He looked back to Alyssum. "I can't really walk," he told her with a guilty look.

"Robert, I know your father wasn't very nice, but you shouldn't be behaving like this."

"I shouldn't, should I? Not a very nice man. You have no idea what kind of man he was."

"I've lived next door to the man my whole twelve years."

"Well, I've had eighteen years with the prick."

"Robert," Alyssum gasped at his language.

"Oh, you're worse."

"Am not." She stood with her hands on her hips.

Robert smiled up at her, loving how cute she looked when she was angry.

"Come on, get up." Alyssum reached out and grabbed his arm. She tugged on his arm until he grumbled and stood. He swayed against her and her arms dove around him to hold him up. Her hands smacked against his back.

"Oww," he howled and pulled away from her.

"What?" Alyssum stared at him with wide, frightened eyes. "What did I do? I only touched your back."

Robert turned white and sat back on the chaise. He only wore his black breeches and boots with a white shirt that wasn't tucked in.

"Robert?" Alyssum sat beside him and placed her hand on his shoulder. "You can tell me anything."

Robert smiled softly. Slowly raising his hands, he began unbuttoning his shirt. Alyssum took her hand back and watched him curiously. "What are you doing?" She arched a brow in confusion.

"Showing you something," he muttered and pulled the shirt off his shoulders.

Robert stood from the chaise and turned his back to her. He winced as he heard her horror-filled gasp.

"What happened?" she demanded as she stood. "Who did this to you?" She stared at the raw, red whip lashes over the expanse of Robert's back.

"Who do you think?" he turned back around and shrugged his shirt back on. He didn't bother re-buttoning it.

"But..." Alyssum shook her head. "He was your father."

"He believed in harsh punishments." He leant down and grabbed the bottle off the floor. "Treading mud on the Persian rug in the foyer was not acceptable," he slurred in anger then moved to take another gulp of liquor.

"Stop that." Alyssum snatched the bottle from him.

"Give that back." He reached for the bottle but she pulled her arm away, keeping him from it. "Alyssum," he warned.

Alyssum stared at him with stubborn eyes then smiled.

"What are you thinking?" he asked cautiously. She raised the bottle high then threw it at the wall. It shattered with a loud smash. Robert stared at the broken glass then looked back at her. "Are you insane?" he breathed.

Alyssum laughed. "Join me," she said as she stepped over to Robert's father prized book collection. She grabbed the priceless books and threw them to the floor. She grabbed one, opened it then ripped out a page. She turned to see Robert staring wide eyed at her. He hadn't even been allowed to touch those books. "Not even a little tempted?" she asked, then shredded another page. "What's he going to do?" She ripped another page, throwing it carelessly behind her.

Robert slowly began to smile. He stepped towards her and took the book from her hand. Without words, they began tearing the office to shreds. Torn books lined the floor. His father's mahogany desk was on its side and its contents were spilled over the floor.

They laughed while destroying the room. Robert turned his head to see Alyssum throw a book into the wall.

"Now what?" She panted as she surveyed the room.

"Dinner." He looked down at her then laughed as he found them both breathless.

Alyssum shook her head. "It's not enough," she muttered and stepped over the wreckage.

"What do you mean, it's not enough?" Robert asked laughing. He had thought to make himself happy by drinking, but in the end all he'd needed was Alyssum. "The place is a mess. My father would be screaming in rage and demanding punishment."

"He's never going to hurt you again."

Robert raised his brows at how angry she sounded. She was practically growling. He frowned as he watched her lean down and pick up a match box.

"Alyssum," he warned.

She turned and shook the box in her hand with a smile.

"That's not funny," he said, but laughed at the same time.

Walking to the corner of the room, Alyssum picked up another bottle of liquor and dropped it on the ripped pages. The liquor spilled from the bottle and ran onto the paper.

"Alyssum," Robert snapped. "Don't." He pointed a finger at her in warning. "We've done enough."

"If he thinks he can hurt you and not be punished in return, he's got another thing coming to him," she said and pulled a match out of the box.

"Alyssum, the man's dead. That's his punishment."

"Not good enough." She whipped the match over the side of the box and lit it.

"Alyssum, put that out."

Alyssum looked up to him and smiled as she dropped the match onto the floor.

Robert jumped forward, but it was too late. The match hit the liquor-coated paper and it went up in flames. Alyssum jumped back with a squeak of surprise. Robert reached her side and yanked her to him.

"Wow, that was quick," Alyssum said as the flames suddenly grew. Robert watched them travel over the rest of the pages. He looked down to his feet and saw he and Alyssum were standing on paper.

"Robert." He could hear the fear in her voice as she noticed the flames were moving too quickly. She jumped as the late Viscount Lambert's mahogany desk went up in a blaze. She grabbed Robert's hand and clutched tight. He held her hand as he moved them backwards. He looked through the flames and saw the door. "Herbert!" he shouted over the roar of the fire.

Soon enough the door opened and Herbert jumped back with fright as flames came towards him. "Fire!" he shouted and ran for help.

Robert looked down and saw the fire was getting closer. "Shit," he whispered.

"Don't swear," Alyssum muttered as she also stared at the fire approaching them.

"Now's not the time to scold me, Alyssum."

"It's always a good time."

Robert turned as they bumped into the window. He released her hand and pushed against it. He cursed when he found it was jammed. Robert turned and scanned the room quickly. He saw a large book untouched by the flames lying on the floor. Running over, he scooped it up before the flames caught it. Alyssum brought her arms up over her face as he threw the book at the window and shattered the glass.

Without thought, he grabbed Alyssum and threw himself along with her out the window.

They landed in a hedge below. Robert rolled out of the hedge then pulled Alyssum out. They both looked up and saw the flames billowing out the window.

"Oops," Alyssum said while staring up.

Robert rubbed his forehead in shock. He was still reeling over what had just happened.

Turning his gaze down, he looked at Alyssum then laughed.

"What?" Alyssum looked at him.

"You're a mess," he laughed and pulled a twig from her unraveling hair.

Sudden shouts turned their gazes.

"Father," Alyssum said to herself and moved around the house.

Robert followed after her, his shirt still hanging open.

"You can't go in there," they heard Herbert yell.

"Alyssum," her father shouted.

"Liss," Harry called out after her father.

She ran along the house, came to the front and called out to them. They turned their heads towards her voice and sighed in relief. Harry then looked behind her at Robert.

"I'm going to kill you." Harry charged at Robert.

Robert moved backwards and held his hands out.

"You two," a commanding voice froze Robert, Alyssum and Harry. "What in the world happened?" James Rosewood demanded. His usual smiling face was stern, his blue eyes livid. He planted his hands on his lean hips. "Well?"

"It was my fault," Robert spoke up. "I was drinking. It was stupid. I lit a fire and it got out of hand. I'm sorry."

Alyssum chewed her bottom lip. Her father turned his gaze to her and saw through the lie.

"Home. Now," he spoke quietly to Alyssum.

Alyssum nodded.

Robert watched Alyssum retreating over the grass, her father following behind her.

"You think my father an idiot?" Harry snapped.

"No," Robert said and looked around him as the servants ran in and out of the house with buckets of water.

"He knows it was Alyssum."

"But I told him—"

"Lies." Harry stared at Robert until he exhaled.

"She'll just get spanked as usual, right?" Robert asked with worry. He knew the earl was a good man who loved his family deeply, he would never hurt them, unlike his own father, but he had never seen the earl so mad.

"I don't know," Harry muttered.

"She'll be fine," Robert told himself. But little did he know it was the last time he would see her for four years. The next morning she had been put into the family's carriage crying and sent to the school in Paris.

Present

"Have you ever told anyone?" Robert watched Alyssum stiffen at the sound of his voice. Robert could no longer hear the chatter of the guests up on the Darrel's terrace. They were all alone in the garden.

"Told them what?" she asked with her back still turned.

"That you burned down my father's office." As he spoke he walked over the grass and stepped into the gazebo.

"No," she replied. "Have you?"

"No." He leaned against the entrance frame. "It's still our secret."

"You almost told my family that night you came to the house drunk."

"Ah." Robert nodded. "Apologies."

"Why this topic of conversation?"

"I was just thinking of the last time I saw you. It was that day wasn't it?"

Alyssum turned with a frown. "You're looking at me right now."

"But you're not the girl who left, nor are you the girl who used to call me by my first name."

"I grew up."

"You got prudish."

"I did not."

"Yes, you did."

"Did not."

"All right, if you're still the same girl then when was the last time you swam in the lake back at the country estate?" She stared at him in silence so he continued baiting her. "Or played in the rain? Had a mud fight?"

"I'm not five anymore," she replied.

"Nor are you any fun."

Alyssum huffed and moved to storm past him, but Robert stood straight and stepped in her way. She took a step back as he came closer.

"Moments ago your hands were on me, now you can't stand near me."

"If someone saw..."

"Right." Robert nodded curtly. "Ruin."

Alyssum kept the proper distance between them. "I'm sure you're quite acquainted with ruin," she snipped tartly.

Robert chuckled. "I am quite acquainted."

"Will you let me pass?"

"No," Robert replied easily and crossed his arms over his chest.

Alyssum let out an aggravated breath.

"All right. I have a solution to our dilemma."

"What dilemma?"

"Regarding how you're going to get past me."

"I wouldn't call it a dilemma, more like arrogance."

Robert smiled. "Call me by my first name," he told her happily.

"What, that's it?"

"That's it. But—" he raised a finger to her, "—say it nicely."

Alyssum rolled her eyes. She took a step towards him and looked up to meet his gaze. "Will you please let me by...Robert?"

Robert twisted his lips and contemplated. "No." He shook his head.

"You said."

"I said say it nicely."

"I did," she snapped.

Robert shook his head with a smile. "No, you didn't. Now try again." He planted his feet apart and leaned down slightly to hear her answer.

"Robert," she clipped. "Will you please let me by?"

"I'm just not feeling the happiness. Try again, Alyssum."

Alyssum's fiery gaze burned him. He quirked a brow and tried not to laugh.

"Will you please let me by?" she asked in her sweetest, sugary voice. "Robert."

Robert's laugh made her forced smile turn into a real one.

"Well, I could argue the fact that that was very fake."

Alyssum gasped and shoved his chest. He laughed louder as he stumbled back a step.

"That's not ladylike." He rubbed his chest.

"Well, you're not behaving like a gentleman." She raised her chin.

"Sweetheart, I never do." He grinned.

Alyssum took another deep, even breath. *Calm yourself. It's just a grin. Keep your hands to yourself.* With a nod, she took a step forward and moved to walk around him and out of the gazebo. Robert suddenly jumped to the side and blocked her path, again.

Alyssum exhaled loudly and looked up. "You said I could pass."

"You took too long to leave. Now we have another dilemma." His smile was gone.

"What is it now?"

"I don't want you to leave."

Deep breaths. "People will start looking for me," she said quietly. "Do you want Harry to find me like this?"

"What, speaking to me? That is what we're doing, isn't it?" He took a step towards her and she took a step back. They slowly moved farther into the gazebo.

"You're standing too close to me," Alyssum whispered.

"This isn't close," he spoke quietly while his eyes bore into hers. "This is." He took a quick step towards her which made her jump backwards. Her back pressed into the frame of the gazebo and Robert pressed into her front. She gasped, unable to control her reaction to feeling him again. She slowly lifted her gaze back to his. "What are you doing?" she asked breathlessly.

"Standing too close to you." His chest pushed against her breasts, causing her to pant lightly. Their thighs were pressed to one another. Alyssum felt him everywhere.

"I don't think you should be standing this close to me," she whispered.

Robert stared at her intently. He lowered his head and her breath caught. His nose brushed hers then he tilted his head to the side. She gasped as his mouth hovered over hers.

"Very bad idea," she told him, her breath fanning his lips.

"Then why does it feel so good?" he murmured.

Alyssum stared at his eyes as he stared at her mouth. She

lowered her gaze slowly to his mouth. Robert raised his arms to let his forearms rest on the wood beside her head.

Caged in his embrace, Alyssum found herself leaning in. He looked into her eyes just before she closed the space between them and pressed her mouth to his. She sighed in pleasure and let her mouth linger on his. How she had missed doing this. Suddenly terrified of how he would react, she pulled away slowly and met his gaze.

"You kissed me," he said in disbelief.

Alyssum cleared her throat and kept a straight face. He wouldn't upset her, even if he laughed at her kiss. "I thought that was what the new deal was to get by you," she snipped.

Robert shook his head, his nose nudging hers. "No, you didn't," he breathed and stared at her too intently.

The gazebo suddenly became very hard to breathe in. Alyssum panted, her eyes wide as she stared at Robert. What had she done? Why had she kissed him? *Because you wanted to, had wanted to since the last time you had.*

"Why did you kiss me?" he asked quietly.

"Because I thought—"

"No, Alyssum," he cut her off and brought his body closer. "Why?"

She tried not to moan as her body aligned with his.

"Why?" he snapped.

She kept quiet.

"Why?" he demanded.

"Because I wanted to," she retorted.

Robert exhaled as his mind swam in disbelief. Alyssum had kissed him. That sweet mouth that loved to snap at him had kissed him gently. The party behind them vanished. It was just him and Alyssum in this gazebo.

With a quick swoop, his mouth caught hers. He groaned. God, how long had he wanted to do this? He lowered his arms from beside her head and framed her face with his hands. He held her for his plundering kiss, stroking his tongue into her hot mouth, licking, coaxing. His kiss became harder, rougher as her arms came around his neck and pulled him closer. His chest crushed against hers, wanting to be as close as possible. As his mouth moved impatiently, greedily, he distantly recognized these kisses. He had felt this mouth beneath his before, had felt this lush, pliant body mold to his. He had heard these soft whimpering moans.

Scarlet.

He gasped against her mouth but didn't stop. Instead he became more ravenous for her. His hands released her face and reached around to grasp her buttocks. She moaned as he gripped her then lifted her. His mouth released hers for a moment as he set her on the railing of the gazebo. He looked into her flushed face and grinned at his discovery.

Before she could stop him, he whisked her fringe back with his hand. He looked at the yellow bruise and remembered Scarlet hitting him. Alyssum leant back and pushed her fringe back down.

"I bumped it," she rushed to explain.

"On my forehead," he replied.

Her eyes widened. "What?"

"You think I wouldn't remember your kiss?" He moved forward for another taste.

Her legs parted for him and he moved between the cradle of her thighs. He ran his fingers over her lips, his gaze over her face, memorizing every feature, even though he already knew every curve and line.

"What are you speaking of?" She pushed his chest and moved to hop down.

Robert gripped her thighs and held her still. His mind was reeling. He was only able to say one thing in answer to her question. "Scarlet."

She didn't move. "I'm not her," she whispered, eyes wide.

"You're a terrible liar." He tangled his hand into her pinned up curls and placing his mouth back to hers. It took her only a moment before she was kissing him back. She wrapped her arms around him, her mouth moving hungrily. Robert moaned in pleasure. He released his grip on her hair and glided his hands downward. He ran his hands down the column of her neck, cupped the round globes of her breasts with a groan then stroked down her stomach.

He took the hem of her gown in his hands and drew the material up. As he raised the material, he smoothed his hands up her legs. He reached her thighs and moaned as his fingers touched bare skin.

"Robert?" Harry's voice called out.

Alyssum and Robert tore apart. She jumped down from the railing and ran from the gazebo. Robert watched her disappear around the back of the hedge. He panted for breath and groaned at his aching shaft. He found his hands were shaking and his heart pounding. He had found her. His Scarlet. And she had been exactly who he had dreamed her to be. Alyssum.

"There you are." Harry stepped around the hedge and came towards the gazebo.

Robert pulled his coat forward, hiding the evidence of his desire for Harry's sister. As Harry stepped up into the gazebo he looked at Robert then exhaled. "Do you know what Miss Darrel would do if she found out you've been ruining a member of her party?"

Robert laughed breathlessly. He could never hide anything from Harry.

"Who was she?" Harry asked.

Robert shook his head with a whoosh of breath.

"That good?" Harry quirked a brow.

"Amazing," Robert answered with a grin.

"Come on, people will soon realize you've been missing." Harry stepped out of the gazebo and Robert followed.

"Does this mean you are letting Scarlet go?" Harry asked cautiously.

"Never," Robert answered as they walked together up the steps of the terrace.

Chapter Eleven

That night, as Alyssum and her family sat at the dining table eating dinner, she could only stare at her food. Robert knew. She had thought he would be horrified, angry, but he had kissed her. Knowing the truth, he had wanted her, or did he want Scarlet?

After returning from the gazebo, Alyssum had kept beside Lilly for the rest of the afternoon and kept her gaze away from Robert.

She distantly heard Harry talking and tuned in.

"...leaving tomorrow."

"What?" she asked quickly.

Harry turned his gaze to her. "I'm leaving tomorrow," he told her.

"You could stay for one more week," Caroline urged softly.

"I've had enough." Harry spoke quietly and Caroline nodded in understanding. Her gaze drifted to her son's cheek where a thin scar lay.

"I'll come with you," Alyssum said.

"What?" Their mother gasped. "You can't."

"I'm not finding a husband this season, Mother."

"But you could, if you bothered to look."

Violet chuckled.

"Don't make me start on you, young lady. You need a husband too."

Violet stopped laughing and looked horrified.

"What about Lord Avery?" Caroline asked Alyssum.

"I wouldn't allow her to marry him," Harry spoke firmly.

"Thank you," Alyssum smiled at Harry while their mother huffed.

"I'll join you two," Violet spoke up and Caroline huffed louder.

"Fine." She threw up her hands and stood. "Never get married. Never give me grandbabies." She left the room in a storm.

"Harry, give Mother a grandbaby," Violet told him.

"You give her a grandchild," he snapped back.

"You're older."

"You're female."

"Oh, you're going to draw that card?" Violet asked with fire in her eyes, a look only her family saw.

Alyssum smiled. "When will we leave?"

Harry turned his gaze slowly from a fuming Violet. "In the morning."

"Early morning or late morning?" Violet asked.

Harry arched a brow and Violet smiled. "Late morning it is," she said, pleased.

"Are you sure you want to leave, Alyssum?" Harry asked. "Lilly will not be pleased."

"She'll forgive me. Plus I've had enough too."

Harry nodded then excused himself, leaving Alyssum alone with Violet. The servants came forward, took the plates and left.

"Are you running from a certain someone?" Violet placed her elbows on the table and rested her chin on her fists.

"No," Alyssum retorted.

"He'll follow you."

"Who?"

Violet gave her a look that said do I look stupid?

"He knows."

Violet raised her brows. "He knows."

"He saw the bruise."

"You bumped it in the kitchen."

"He said I bumped it on his forehead."

"More like slammed it," Violet muttered. "Has Harry seen the bruise?"

"No."

Violet looked at Alyssum's wispy fringe. "Mother?" she asked.

"No," Alyssum answered.

"We'll have to wait and see."

"For what?"

"To see if he'll come after you."

"Who—"

"Stop that. We both know of whom we are speaking."

Alyssum sighed. "Do you think he'll follow?" she asked, hesitant.

"I saw you two in the gazebo. He'll follow," announced Violet.

"You saw?" Alyssum gasped.

"I had my eye on that gazebo first."

Alyssum shook her head, speechless. "What did you see?"

Violet arched a brow as her cheeks turned pinkish. Alyssum exhaled in mortification then dropped her head into her hands with a groan.

"It looked like fun," Violet said quietly.

Alyssum laughed and kept her head in her hands.

"Was it?"

Alyssum raised her head. She stared at Violet for a moment before sighing. "Yes."

"Thought so," Violet muttered.

Robert took a deep breath before knocking on the Rosewood's door. He turned his head to look at a carriage roll by. In the middle of the day the streets were bustling.

When no one answered the door, he knocked more loudly.

Hopefully Harry wouldn't kill him when he announced he wanted to marry Alyssum. With any luck, it will only be one punch, perhaps two, then he could see Alyssum. But asking Alyssum to marry him terrified him more than facing Harry. He could take a punch to the face or the gut, but to the heart? That bruise might not fade. He would be strong and if she moved to run he would just pin her down and wait till she said yes. With that thought, he smiled.

When the front door opened, he took another a deep breath and announced to the butler that he wanted to speak to the Earl of Leighton.

"He's not here," the butler informed him.

"Is Lady Alyssum?"

"They left, sir."

"What?" Robert snapped in confusion.

"They traveled back to the country estate this morning."

"Why?" He took a quick step forward and the young butler jumped back in fright.

"Don't know, sir."

Robert growled in anger and hurried back to his own townhouse.

"Otis," he yelled for his butler when he stormed inside.

"Yes, sir." The old man scurried forward.

"Ready my horse and pack my bags. I want a light travel bag for my journey and send the rest of my things after me," he snapped out orders.

"Where are you off to, sir?"

"My country estate," he grumbled and strode up the stairs towards his room.

A knock on the door made him pause on the staircase and turn. He waited to see who it was as Otis opened the door. "Jackson." He watched Jackson stride in to the foyer.

"Lambert." Jackson grinned. His grin slipped as he saw the anger in Robert's face.

"Didn't go well, huh?" He knew Robert had been going to Harry's to talk to him, but Robert hadn't told him what it had been about.

"They weren't there."

"So wait."

"Until they come back to town?" Robert snapped sarcastically.

"Pardon?"

"They left town. They went back to their country estate."

"Oh."

"Sir," a maid called from the top of the stairs. Robert and Jackson both looked up. "Your traveling bag is ready," she said, out of breath.

"Thank you."

"Going somewhere?" Jackson asked.

"She thinks she can run from me."

"Alyssum always seemed like a runner."

Robert mumbled in agreement then frowned. He turned his gaze to Jackson and stared at him in question.

Jackson chuckled. "Took you long enough to figure it out."

"You knew it was her?"

"I wasn't sure until the night at the theatre."

Robert shook his head, taking it all in. "But when—"

"Maybe we could talk on the way?" Jackson asked.

"On the way?" Robert frowned.

"I wouldn't mind visiting the countryside, see what the fuss is about." Jackson grinned.

Five minutes later, Robert and Jackson were galloping out of town, their horses leaving a dust cloud behind them.

"Alyssum?"

Alyssum looked up from her gardening.

"Are you being careful?" Violet asked as she approached Alyssum where she worked on the rose bush at the side of the house.

"Yes." Alyssum smiled even though her finger still ached as it healed underneath her work gloves

"Mother said it's time for you to come in. Dinner will be served soon and you should wash up." Violet looked at Alyssum dirt-smudged face.

Alyssum sighed as she stood and picked up the basket of cut roses and her tools.

"How have you been?" Violet asked as they walked towards the back entrance of the house. "You've been quiet since our return yesterday."

"I've just got a lot on my mind."

"Like a certain viscount?"

Alyssum laughed quietly as they stepped into the house and closed the door behind them.

"We've been back for a whole day and..."

"And he's not here," Violet finished for her. "He may have wanted to give you some time."

Alyssum shrugged and placed her basket of roses on the kitchen bench.

"I have to go get ready for dinner." Alyssum walked by Violet and up the kitchen stairs.

That night during dinner, Harry, Violet, Alyssum and Caroline kept turning their gazes to the gossiping maids in the corner. They spoke quickly and quietly, sometimes giggling.

When they both suddenly giggled louder, Harry exhaled and turned his gaze to them.

"What is it?" he asked them.

When the maids saw it was Harry who had spoken, they both fell silent and stood straight against the wall.

"Speak!"

"Ladies, if you please," Caroline said gently.

The short one out of the two stepped up and bobbed in a curtsey. "Ah, there was news from the Lambert estate."

Alyssum and Violet both shared a glance across the table then looked back to the maid.

"What is it?" Harry asked now appearing concerned.

"Viscount Lambert was spotted by the gardener riding towards his estate. Another gentleman was with him, but what caught the gardener's attention was how fast they were riding." The maid became louder and more excited. "He said it was like they were running from the devil himself."

"Thank you, Bethany." Caroline nodded. "So Robert has returned to the country. Any ideas on why?"

Harry shook his head while a crease furrowed his brow.

Alyssum looked up to Violet and watched as she smiled at her brightly. She felt like she was going to faint. Maybe Robert just wanted to visit the countryside. Maybe there was something wrong with his estate and he had to return quickly. Or was he here for her? That thought made her belly flutter with nerves and her body warm.

"I hope nothing's wrong," Caroline said. "Harry, did Robert say anything that would cause worry?"

"Uh, no," Harry muttered then concentrated on the food before him.

Caroline frowned then took a sip of wine from her glass.

The table was silent and even the maids held their tongues. Alyssum ate mechanically while her mind pulled her to her room and under her bed where a white box lay hidden, taunting her.

That night, after excusing herself, Alyssum lay in bed staring at the ceiling. She felt her whole world spinning. She saw her masked gentlemen kissing her on the balcony, Robert revealing himself. She remembered how she'd wanted to kiss him every time she'd seen him or spoken to him, then finally kissing him at the tavern. Out of all those events, what burned in her mind the most was the afternoon in the gazebo at Lilly's luncheon. There had been no masks, no hiding. They had just kissed, as Alyssum and Robert.

Chapter Twelve

Back and forth. Back and forth. Alyssum treaded over the soft grass beneath her feet in long strides. Her mind had been reeling but was now blank. All that her mind said was, *back and forth, back and forth. Don't think of Robert, just think of the grass beneath your feet and walking over it.*

It was now midday and there was still no sign of Robert.

"Harrumph." Alyssum stomped her foot and stopped pacing. The house was out of sight from where she stood in the trees separating the Leighton estate and the Lambert's. She faced the house and thought of going back. He may have come. But he usually rode or walked through his estate and onto theirs. He didn't take the main road. She took a deep breath, hefting her chest then exhaling loudly.

"Something on your mind?"

A wave of warmth and lust washed over her body and settled low in her belly. Robert.

Taking another breath, she turned slowly and faced him. His usual rumpled appearance caused her cravings to spiral out of control. His cheeks were darkened with stubble and she yearned to kiss his soft lips.

"Good morning," she managed to say.

A grin curved his lips. He looked down as he took a step forward then brought his gaze back to hers. The amusement in his eyes slipped away as he stared at her. "Why did you leave?"

Alyssum felt she couldn't breathe under his dark gaze. His

voice was low, alluring.

"Harry wanted to return," she informed him.

"And you couldn't stay with your mother and sister?"

"We all wanted to return."

"Terrible liar," he muttered as he dropped his gaze to the ground and took another step forward. As he raised his eyes and caught hers again, he asked, "Why...did you leave?"

He was getting too close. "I don't like the city," she answered.

"You should have come to me. I would have persuaded you to stay."

"It was a sudden decision."

"One that was made the same day you kissed me."

"You kissed me," she argued.

"You kissed me first." His grin came back and he took another step forward. He now stood before her, the toes of his boots an inch from her walking boots. "Have you forgotten that?" he asked. "I haven't. It was very sweet and not at all innocent."

"If you're trying to say I'm not an innocent then I suggest we go to the house and you can say that again in front of Harry."

Robert laughed, his eyes lightening. "Well played," he murmured. "How's the forehead?" He raised his hand to move her fringe aside. Alyssum batted his fingers aside.

"It's fine."

"Knocked it in the kitchen, eh?"

"Yes."

"You sure about that? Are you sure you didn't sneak into The Dove at night, go into a room...and wait for me?"

"Yes," she breathed.

"*Tsk, tsk.* Terrible liar." He moved fast. His step took up the space between them and then his arms were around her waist, lifting her. He set her down on a fallen tree. Her face was now level with his. Hands on either side of her thighs, he leaned in, his face close to hers.

Alyssum sat frozen as she stared at him.

"I'm not letting you move from this spot till you tell me the truth."

Her mouth remained stubbornly shut.

"You bought a dress. I assume that's how it all began?"

Alyssum's eyes widened a degree as he spoke.

"Tricked your family by faking a headache then came to Lady Brook's ball in a scarlet gown. Am I getting close?" He moved nearer, his breath fanning her lips as his eyes burned into hers with the want for truth. "Turned my world upside down with a kiss then kneed me in a very unladylike manner."

Alyssum swallowed.

"You want your garter back...Scarlet?"

Alyssum gasped then oh so slowly shook her head.

"Why did you do it?" he asked quietly. Alyssum's mouth moved but no words came.

"Did you know it was me?" he asked.

She shook her head again.

"Why did you come to the tavern?" he asked in a low voice.

Robert had wanted the answer to that question ever since he had known it Alyssum was Scarlet, ever since he had kissed her in the gazebo.

"Why did you come to the tavern?" he asked louder, firmer. She remained silent.

187

At Lady Brook's she had kissed a masked stranger and when he had revealed himself she had kneed him, not unveiled herself. But then she had come to The Dove. She had come to him.

He needed her to tell him why.

"Alyssum, why did you come to the tavern?" he asked. "Why?" he shouted when she remained silent.

"Because I wanted to kiss you again," she shouted and then went silent. Her mouth closed, eyes wide in horror at the slip of her tongue.

Robert exhaled on a laugh. He raised his hand from the tree and gripped her nape, bringing her closer to him. "You could have just asked," he whispered against her lips.

"You wanted Scarlet," she spoke sadly. "Not Alyssum."

Robert smiled. "Alyssum, you are Scarlet."

Alyssum dropped her eyes to his lips.

"Do you want to ask me something now?" he asked.

"No," she murmured while staring at his mouth.

"Liar," he chuckled then moved in. He brushed his lips over hers then moved away. Alyssum swayed forward. Robert grinned and moved forward again, brushing her lips with his. He lost himself in her kiss. He tightened his hand on her nape and slanted his mouth firmly over hers. He felt her gasp then reach up her hands and hold his shoulders. She arched her back, pushing herself against him. Her mouth met his, ever demanding. Ravenous, they kissed with complete abandon.

"Aw, you two made up," a voice reached them through the pleasure.

Alyssum shoved Robert's chest and he moved back with a groan of reluctance.

Robert turned with a hard glare and stared at Jackson. "I'm

so glad you chose to tag along."

"Me too." Jackson grinned. "Alyssum." He winked at her flushed face.

Robert felt Alyssum squirming behind him as she tried to slip off the tree. He turned and helped her down and she took a step back while brushing off her green day dress.

"Or should I call you Scarlet?" Jackson asked.

"Jackson," Robert warned.

"Alyssum it is. So did you accept Robert's proposal?"

Robert's eyes popped wide, as did Alyssum's.

Robert glared at Jackson fiercely. His glare promised pain. Jackson smiled.

Robert had announced last night that he wanted to marry Alyssum. After a few drinks, Jackson had gotten him to slip out more information about how much he wanted and always had wanted Alyssum, even knowing Harry would kill him for lusting after his sister.

"What?" Alyssum asked.

"What?" Jackson asked with an obviously fake look of confusion on his face.

Robert turned to Alyssum and cleared his throat.

Alyssum's eyebrows rose high. The man had jumped off a bridge and into the Thames half naked. He wasn't scared of anything. And yet he was nervous about voicing his next words.

"Alyssum." He cleared his throat again. "I would like to speak to you alone."

Alyssum looked over to Jackson who winked and nodded.

Robert placed his arms behind his back and hid the fact he was clutching his hands for dear life.

Alyssum felt dizzy. First his kiss then a certain proposal. How could they expect her to stand? Was the proposal marriage? What else would it be? He wouldn't dare offer her to be his mistress, not if he liked bedding women.

"Um," was all she was able to say. She was stunned.

"Robert," Harry shouted, suddenly appearing over the lawn.

Robert swung around and watched as Harry approached them. "Harry." He nodded to his best friend.

"Jackson," Harry said surprised as he saw him. "What are you doing in the country?"

"I thought I would get some fresh air."

Harry frowned but nodded. "Alyssum, Mother's looking for you."

"Oh." She skirted her gaze to Robert then back to Harry. "Now?"

"Yes."

Alyssum nodded then slowly walked by Robert and then Harry on her trip back to the house.

"I was on my way to see you," she heard Harry tell Robert.

Alyssum closed the front door and fell back on to it with a puff of breath.

"You look utterly flushed, my dear," Caroline announced as she walked out of the front parlor and into the foyer. "Long walk?"

"Yes," Alyssum exhaled then stood away from the door. "Harry said you were looking for me."

"Yes, you were nowhere to be found. I was worried."

"I woke up early and decided to go for a walk. It's good to be back in the country." She smiled.

"I'm sorry I interrupted your walk."

Alyssum shook her head. "It doesn't matter."

Caroline smiled then walked back into the front parlor. When her mother was out of sight, Alyssum walked quickly towards the library. She entered and closed the doors behind her.

Hearing the library door close, Violet poked her head over the first shelf.

"Alyssum."

Alyssum turned around and frowned when she could not see Violet. She looked up and found her.

"Come down," Alyssum waved impatiently.

Violet made a noise of irritation but disappeared behind the shelf as she walked down the ladder.

Alyssum waited with a franticly beating heart until Violet reappeared.

"What's the matter?" Violet asked as she walked around the bookshelf and sat on a leather high back chair. "You're all red," she said.

Alyssum exhaled and sat herself beside Violet. They turned in their seats to look at one another.

"What have you been up to, Alyssum?" Violet asked suspiciously.

"I was walking, then I saw Robert."

Violet nodded.

"He definitely knows."

"That you're Scarlet."

"Yes."

"Well, it's about time," Violet gushed and leant back on her seat.

"We...um...we..." Alyssum chewed her bottom lip.

"Did you kiss him again?"

Alyssum nodded.

"Is that why you're red?"

"I don't know," Alyssum exclaimed frantically. "I just am." She placed her hands on her burning cheeks.

"Okay. Calm down." Violet urged her.

"Mr. West saw us."

"Jackson?"

"Mr. West."

Violet rolled her eyes.

"Don't do that. It's rude."

Violet rolled her eyes again and Alyssum exhaled sharply.

"Alyssum, deep breaths," Violet recommended. "Now tell me what's wrong?"

Alyssum took a deep long breath then exhaled. "Mr. West mentioned something about a proposal," she exclaimed.

Violet stared at her, looking confused.

"After he caught me and Robert..." Alyssum was at a loss for words so she decided to skip that part. "He asked if I'd accepted Robert's proposal. What could that mean?"

"It could mean many things. First of all, remain calm."

Alyssum nodded quickly.

"I see by the look on your face you're thinking marriage."

"Well, what kind of other proposals are there?"

"Business."

"Business?"

"Yes."

"Why would Robert want to propose a business deal with

me?"

Violet shrugged. Alyssum calmed down and frowned as she thought about different proposals.

"What if he does want to propose marriage?"

"Violet, you're not helping."

"Well, would it be so bad to marry Robert?"

"Yes."

"Why?" Violet demanded.

"You know Robert. He would want to live in London and I want to live here where it's quiet. Robert loves crowds and *soirées*. I hide in quiet spots at *soirées*. And we all know his reputation with women. He would never remain faithful to one woman." Alyssum huffed in anger.

Violet stared quietly. "But we don't know what he would do for love."

"I'm sorry I interrupted your reading," she said before she stood and walked from the library.

Alyssum dragged her feet as she climbed the stairs and made her way to her room.

Sitting on the edge of her bed slowly, she stared ahead at nothing as she thought about Violet's question. What if he does want to propose marriage?

What if he did? Would she say yes? No? Maybe?

Did she want to marry Robert? He drove her insane. They fought constantly. They would kill each other.

Alyssum dropped back onto the bed and stared at the ceiling. She thought about the times they snipped at each other. She had always felt exhilarated and alive while insulting him. He was able to make her feel happier and more beautiful than anyone had ever tried to accomplish. She loved him.

Alyssum sat up bolt straight. "Blimey," she gasped. Yes. If Robert proposed marriage she would say yes. And she would keep him forever, for herself, never to share him with another.

Alyssum exhaled then stood. Her gaze lowered to under the bed where the white box filled with the scarlet gown lay. With a small smile tugging the corners of her lips, she walked over to the bell pull and called Meg.

"Yes, miss?" The maid said as she entered.

"Can you please get Violet for me?"

Meg nodded then slipped from the room, shutting the door behind her.

Alyssum dropped to her knees once the door closed and reached under the bed. When her fingers grasped the box, she pulled it out. Her small smile turned into a bright, happy one as she stared down at the white box.

Violet gasped in surprise as she walked into Alyssum's room. "What are you doing?" she whispered and stared at Alyssum, or rather Scarlet.

"Please cover for me if anyone asks where I've gone." Alyssum stood before her in the scarlet gown, her hair unbound.

"What am I suppose to say?"

"Just tell them I went for a walk." Alyssum picked up her black mask.

"Liss, what are you doing?"

Alyssum paused and looked at Violet. "We're finally going to talk about this."

"And you need to wear that dress to do that?"

Alyssum bit her bottom lip then wound the black domino around her face. She tied the ends and dropped her hands to her sides with a sigh.

"You better hope Mother and Harry don't see you like this," Violet warned.

"Are you sure Harry has returned?"

"I heard him speaking to Mother a moment ago in the drawing room."

"That's what you're here for. You're my eyes and ears." Alyssum grabbed her black cloak and drew it around her.

"You owe me." Violet turned and opened the door. Alyssum drew up her hood then stepped up behind Violet.

"All clear," Violet whispered and they both began creeping their way to the back entrance of the house.

"Wait," Violet whispered quickly and watched as their chef bustled around the kitchen.

"When I give you the signal, you run for the door," Violet whispered.

"What's the signal?" Alyssum asked but Violet had already walked into the kitchen.

"Good afternoon, Coralene," Violet said happily as she stood before the chef.

"Lady Violet." Coralene smiled. "What can I do for you?"

"I was wondering if you had any of those scrumptious cookies you make?"

Coralene's round cheeks glowed with happiness. "Why yes, miss, right over here." Coralene made her way to a jar sitting on the bench.

Violet turned towards the kitchen door and waved her arms frantically at Alyssum.

Alyssum took that as the sign and ran through the kitchen and out the back door.

Alyssum exhaled then pushed away from the door. She crossed the lawn and walked quickly towards the Lambert estate. She crossed into the trees and began skirting around broken logs. She walked along the path until she reached the clearing of Robert's estate.

She took a breath for courage then took off her cloak, laid it over her arm and strode purposely towards the front door.

Robert turned his head towards the knock on his office door. He sat before his desk with his feet propped up.

"Come in," he called and hoped it wasn't Jackson.

The door opened to reveal Robert's young butler.

"Sir, you have a caller," he announced.

Robert grumbled. "Who?"

His butler fidgeted before answering. "I'm not quite sure. It's a lady," he said knowingly.

"Back one day and the horde moves in," Robert muttered. He dropped his head back on his chair. "Tell her I'm not here."

"Ah." His butler fidgeted again then left.

Robert relaxed back in his chair then groaned as a knock came at the door again.

"Just send her away," he called out.

The door opened and Robert turned his head again, expecting to see his butler. He felt his jaw drop when Scarlet walked in.

"Should I leave?" Alyssum asked.

"No." Robert jumped up from his seat. He stumbled as he

dove for the door and moved to shut it. "Do *not* tell Mr. West we have a guest," he ordered his butler then shut the door and turned to Alyssum. He let out a slow breath as he saw her clearly for the first time. He had always seen Scarlet at night, but now in the day he saw her clearly and it was without a doubt Alyssum. Her green eyes, her lips, her jaw, her stubborn chin.

Alyssum turned to her side and laid her cloak over the chaise before turning back to Robert.

"So, here I am, Scarlet. You finally found her. Now what?" Alyssum asked, trying to keep her voice strong and not shaky and breathless.

"Now I'm going to do something I've wanted to do for a long time." Robert stepped forward and Alyssum felt a wave of heat spread through her body. He reached out and untied her mask. She smiled. He removed the mask and smiled down at her as he dropped it atop her cloak.

"You struck me. Twice." Robert smiled in amusement.

"I'm sorry about that," Alyssum whispered. "You kept trying to take my mask off."

"I wanted to know who you were."

"I didn't want you to know."

"Why?" Robert asked, curious.

"I thought you would be angry and...disappointed."

"Disappointed. Does it look like I'm disappointed?" He took a step closer to her brushing his chest against her breasts.

"Um," she murmured, at a loss for words.

"Does it feel like I'm disappointed?" he whispered and brushed his lower body against hers with a grin. Alyssum's cheeks burned as she felt him hard and eager against her belly.

"I came here to talk," she said sternly.

Robert chuckled. "Then you shouldn't have worn this dress." He ran his gaze slowly down her body, over the scarlet gown.

"Robert, now is not the time to act like a rake. We need to talk. You need to... mmm." She was cut off by Robert's ardent kiss. He tunneled his hands into her hair, holding her to him as his mouth pressed firmly against hers. He released her mouth but kept hold of her. Her breath panted harshly against his grinning lips.

"I was speaking," she snapped. "It's ru—" She groaned as Robert cut her off again with another kiss.

He pulled back smiling. "I've wanted to do that every time you talked back to me."

"Really?" she asked surprised.

"Really." He leant forward, but this time as their lips met the kiss was soft and gentle. He coaxed her into the kiss, drawing her in with light licks of his tongue and nips with his teeth.

Alyssum sighed and fell against his body. She looped her arms around his neck and opened her mouth eagerly for him. Robert wound his arms around her waist and held her to him as he slowly melted her with his mouth. Her neck arched back as his mouth traveled across her cheek and over her jaw. She clenched her hands into his jacket as he kissed her collarbone and ran his hands up her sides.

For years he had been her best friend. Then she had lost him for four while at school, and because of her own stubbornness she had lost him for another six. But now he was hers.

He lowered her down onto the chaise. She tangled her

hands into his hair and held him tight as she met his kiss. He ran his hands up her legs, raising the material of her skirt along the way. His hands on her knees, he parted her legs and urged her to wrap them around him. Their breathing became ragged as he settled into the cradle of her thighs and pressed against her. Alyssum broke from the kiss with a cry of pleasure. Robert's gaze blazed as he stared at her while rocking between her thighs, causing her to gasp and moan. Alyssum gripped his jacket as her body went up in flames and burned for him.

She shoved his jacket from his shoulders and he shrugged out of it. As it hit the floor Alyssum was already untying his cravat and tossing it aside. Both their hands dove for the buttons on his waistcoat and shirt. Robert pulled off the waistcoat then his shirt. His hands clasped her fingers and tugged off her long glove. Alyssum gave him her other hand. This time he took his time, pulling the silk glove away slowly. He dropped it to the floor then gasped in pleasure as her bare hands touched his chest.

Alyssum felt herself smiling as she watched Robert's eyes close in response to her caress.

He placed his hands over hers then his body came down on her. He stroked her cheek before laying his lips upon hers. The kiss was slow and languid. As he glided his tongue into her mouth, he reached his hands down and flipped off her slippers. She gave a gasp of surprise as he touched her stocking-clad feet and ran his hands up her long legs. When he reached the top of her stockings, he slid his fingers under the silk and pulled them down her legs, leading a burning path of pleasure. He reached around his back where her legs wrapped and tugged the stockings from her. After dropping them on the floor beside the chaise, he ran his hands back over her bare thighs and sighed.

His kiss became deeper, stronger. He smoothed his hands around her back and tugged at the buttons of her dress. When

199

the row was undone, he tugged and slipped the dress forward. Alyssum gasped and gripped his hands, stopping him from removing the dress.

"I don't...this dress doesn't allow..." she stuttered uncontrollably. "There's..."

Robert grinned and tugged the dress again. "I know," he whispered and Alyssum blushed furiously. She was naked under the gown. The style didn't allow her to wear a shift.

Obviously seeing her falter, Robert swooped down and caught her mouth with his. In seconds, she was moaning and arching up to him. Her hands went lax and he wrenched the gown down. It gathered about her waist. Alyssum gasped as her breasts were bared. Robert moved back and looked at her. He groaned then kissed her again, harder this time. She whimpered and arched into his touch when he palmed her breasts and massaged her nipples.

Alyssum shuddered and slid her hands down his stomach, reveling in the feel of his warm, naked skin. She reached his breeches and slid lower, feeling his lower body move against her. She heard Robert groan as he moved to kiss her neck. She tightened her legs around him in pleasure as he sucked on her neck and rocked his erection between her thighs.

"Robert," she whispered shakily and gripped his hips. The sensitive flesh between her thighs pulsed with need. Each push of his hard flesh against her sent her toes curling. With a yearning to feel him, she slipped her hands between them and cupped his shaft in her hands.

She gasped as he moaned wildly and pushed into her palms.

"Alyssum," he groaned and caught her hands. "Do you know what you are doing?" His eyes were dark and searing as they gazed down at her.

"Not really," she admitted meekly while learning the feel of him with her fingertips.

Robert groaned then shuddered as her hands squeezed around him. "You're doing a pretty good job for not really knowing what you're doing," he said as his eyes grew heavy and a red flush heated his cheeks.

Alyssum smiled at the compliment. "You like this?" she asked and squeezed again.

Robert shouted in pleasure then moved back quickly as he felt himself about to come. "Jesus, woman," he laughed and reined in his release. "You're going to get it now," he growled and lowered his head to her breast and suckled her nipple deep into his mouth.

Alyssum gasped then gave a stunned cry of pleasure. "Oh my," she whispered in awe as she squirmed beneath him. Robert chuckled and moved to her other breast. She clutched his shoulders in a bruising grip as he tugged her nipple then sucked. She didn't mean to, but she screamed.

She moved her fingers back to his shaft. He brought his hand over hers and taught her how to rub him.

His harsh breathing fanned her breast as she rubbed his hard length. Alyssum's body tingled as he ran his hands over her bare legs. She felt herself wanting something so much more as he laid his palms over her inner thighs. She arched her hips wantonly, hardly believing she wanted him to touch her more intimately.

"Please don't tell me to stop," he breathed raggedly in her ear as she felt his hand touch her wet core. She gasped then moaned as he moved his fingers. She didn't want him to stop.

His fingers delved into the slick heat of her feminine core and she cried out in pleasure and clutched his back. His fingers left her and rubbed her slickness over her. He rubbed a spot that caused her thighs to squeeze around him tight and a scream to escape her lips.

"Robert." Her body writhed, burned, urged him for more.

"Don't tell me to stop," he pleaded with her again as he bit her lobe.

"I won't," she gasped and turned her face into his neck to breathe in his warm scent.

She felt a push between her thighs and frowned in confusion.

"Ah," she cried out at the quick pinch of pain she felt as Robert suddenly thrust inside her. She froze. He groaned wildly against her ear and held still. Alyssum's eyes were wide. Did he just? Was he?

She gasped as she felt him move inside her. The pinch of pain subsided. Now all she felt was an ache she didn't understand. Tangling her hands into Robert's hair, she stopped him from nibbling on her ear, which was making her squirm in pleasure. She raised his gaze to hers. Seeing his eyes were heavy and dark, she cupped his face and smoothed her thumbs over his parted lips. A sheen of sweat misted his face. He groaned deeply then leaned down and kissed her. He kissed her deep, hard, stealing the breath from her. She slid her hands into his hair and clutched tightly as he rocked inside her. Her moan of shocked pleasure was muffled by his kiss. He slowly moved his hips back and forth, gliding in and out of her, letting her become accustomed to the feel of him. The ache inside her grew more intense, making her desperate for something.

"Does this hurt?" he whispered against her lips.

"No," she gasped and squeezed her thighs around him.

A look of relief washed over Robert's face and his thrusts became firmer, deeper, making her cry out. When her hands clutched his back and she arched to meet every slick thrust,

Robert let go of his restraint.

One of his hands clutched her nape as the other held her hip. He moved with powerful strokes, rocking her hips with his. Their breath mingled as their bodies rubbed against one another.

Alyssum felt herself growing hotter and a sheen of sweat covered her body. With each stroke of his body, his chest brushed against her nipples, causing sparks of ecstasy to shoot down to where they were joined, making her pleasure greater.

With a harsh groan, Robert pushed Alyssum's legs wider with his knees and thrust faster. She screamed and he clutched her nape and hip and thrust harder. He stared into her eyes while she clamped around him then pulsated as her orgasm erupted inside her.

Alyssum squeezed her eyes shut against the pleasure. Her legs gripped Robert tight and she screamed in amazement. Her body soared and exploded in euphoria. She gasped against the sensations washing over her body and felt herself slowly coming down. She distantly heard Robert shout hoarsely then felt him still inside her. With a loud, heavy exhale, he collapsed over her damp body. Alyssum kept her arms wrapped around him as she regained her breath. She caressed her fingers idly over his sweat beaded back.

"Robert?" she whispered against his hair.

"Mmm," he mumbled.

"Was that...did we just?" He chuckled and she gasped as she still felt him inside her.

"Yes," he murmured. Then with a groan he lifted his head and look at her. "We just had sex."

"Oh," she whispered

"And that was great sex." He moaned as he leant in and

placed a soft kiss to her lips. "You've exhausted me." He grinned.

Alyssum gasped as he slid from her body. She missed his heat instantly. As if knowing just how she felt, Robert lowered back over her body, pressing into her soft curves and placed his face between her breasts with a long sigh.

She smiled and began running her hands up and down his back, her fingers tracing the crisscrossed scars.

Robert turned his head to the side and listened to Alyssum's pounding heartbeat. He lightly grazed his fingers over her nipple and smiled as her heart jumped. His eyes closed in pleasure as she ran her hands over his back. He had wanted her touch for years.

"When did you take your breeches off?" Alyssum asked.

He smiled and looked down at himself. He still wore his boots and breeches. They were just tugged over his hips.

"I got a little impatient," he told her with a smile. He rose over her, his gaze on her flushed cheeks, swollen lips, her long hair flowing around her on the chaise. "Have I ever told you I think you're beautiful?"

Alyssum smiled. "No."

"Well, I do, very much." He lowered himself and kissed her smiling lips. As he moved back, Alyssum caught his face between her hands and kept his mouth on hers. They kissed slowly then pulled back with smiles on their faces.

A loud rattling knock came at the door. Robert looked towards the noise with a frown as Alyssum gasped in fright.

"My butler won't come in without permission," he assured her. She nodded, but then they both jumped in surprise as the knock came again. This time Robert swore the person kicked the door.

"What?" he snapped.

"Harry!" Robert heard Jackson call out from on the other side of the door.

"Shit," Robert exploded and dove off Alyssum. Alyssum gave a small cry as she jumped from the chaise and pulled her dress up over her breasts. She pulled the sleeves up and reached around the back to try and fasten it. She fumbled in her haste.

"I can't button my dress," she said frantically. "Did you break the buttons?"

"Maybe," Robert muttered as he picked up his shirt and pulled it on. They darted their gazes to the door as they heard Harry's mumbled voice on the other side, talking to Jackson.

The door then opened and in walked Harry.

Everyone froze, eyes wide, mouths parted. Jackson stood in the hall outside the room, gave a sympathetic look to Robert then ducked out of view.

Harry's stunned eyes stared at Alyssum. He took in her scarlet gown, her disheveled, unbound hair, her flushed cheeks. He slowly turned a murderous gaze to Robert who stood only wearing his breeches, boots and his unfastened shirt. Sweat misted his skin and he was just as flushed as Alyssum. Harry must have noticed how they were both out of breath.

"Harry," Robert spoke calmly. He put his hands out towards Harry, warding him off. "Remain calm and let me explain."

"Is Alyssum Scarlet?" Harry said quietly.

Alyssum stood frozen, unable to move as she saw how furious Harry was.

"Yes," Robert answered. "But please let me explain."

"No," Harry said in a deadly voice and stepped forward.

Robert turned and ran for the window with Harry chasing after him.

Robert yanked the window open and dove out, straight into the hedges surrounding the house. He rolled off the hedge and onto the drive, his boots kicking up dirt as he ran. He heard Alyssum's shout then heard Harry chasing after him.

"Jackson!" Alyssum screamed as she ran out of the office, holding the bodice of her dress for the back wasn't buttoned and it was falling down.

"I had nothing to do with Harry's appearance," Jackson defended himself quickly from where he stood in the foyer.

"Help me," she ordered.

"I'm staying out of this one."

Alyssum paused at the door to turn and give Jackson the same murderous look Harry had given Robert.

"All right." Jackson sighed and moved forward.

They ran down the front steps and around to the side of the house.

They both paused as they saw Robert and Harry running around a small hedge. Harry changed directions and Robert skidded to a halt then ran the other way.

Alyssum ran forward with a chuckling Jackson behind her. Before Alyssum could stop them, Harry dove over the waist-high hedge and tackled Robert to the grass.

"Stop it," Alyssum shouted as Harry punched Robert.

As they rolled on the grass Harry hit Robert again before Robert managed to shove Harry off him. But before Robert could make a run for it, Harry grasped his boot and tripped him.

"Harry, enough," Alyssum shouted.

Robert hit the grass with a whoosh of breath and Harry scrambled over and threw another punch. This punch landed solidly between Robert's legs.

Robert howled in pain and curled onto his side, cupping himself and cursing profoundly. Alyssum panted for breath as she reached them. Harry stood to his feet and ignored Alyssum as she smacked his arm.

Jackson reached them too and looked down at Robert. But when Alyssum moved forward for Robert, Harry grabbed her arm and held her back.

"Let go," she ordered.

"You're coming home with me," he said angrily. "Now."

"No."

"Alyssum, now is not the time," he growled furiously. "Now move it." As he spoke, he took off his coat and drew it around Alyssum.

Alyssum slipped into it silently. She looked over to Jackson, who nodded and waved her away. Robert groaned and rolled to his knees.

"Haven't had enough, huh?" Harry moved towards him and Alyssum jumped in front of him.

"Stop it," she yelled.

"It's all right, Alyssum," Robert groaned.

"You don't talk to her." Harry pointed a warning finger at him while stepping before Alyssum again. "Ever. You don't come near her, or my family. Understand?"

"No." Robert refused to cower. He raised his chin, defying Harry while kneeling on the grass and cupping his injured manhood.

Harry pulled back his arm and punched Robert again. Alyssum squealed and covered her eyes as Robert hit the grass unconscious. Harry shook his pained hand then turned to Alyssum.

"Let's go." He grabbed her arm.

Alyssum pulled against his hold as she looked at Robert lying still on the grass. She went to argue but saw Jackson shaking his head at her with a stern expression. She sighed deeply then allowed Harry to pull her away.

"Upstairs. Now," Harry ordered as he slammed the front door shut behind them.

"Stop ordering me around." Alyssum pulled her arm free.

"Go change out of that dress."

"No."

"Now, Alyssum. Then I want to talk to you. You'll meet me in my office..." He stopped, anger crossing his face as he obviously remembered walking in on Robert and his sister in an office. "Meet me in the front parlor."

"You didn't have to hurt him."

"Alyssum, please. Go. Change."

"Oh my," her mother exclaimed as she walked into the foyer and ran her gaze over Alyssum, taking in her rumpled appearance, scarlet dress and Harry's coat. "Oh my, my, my." She shook her head.

Alyssum turned bright red and pulled Harry's coat tighter around her. Violet stepped into the foyer beside their mother. Her eyes widened in shock as she looked at Alyssum. Alyssum then moved willingly up the stairs and to her bedroom to change.

Once inside her bedroom, she dropped Harry's coat then her dress to the floor. She stepped over the material and walked to the wash area. She stood behind the screen and poured water into the light blue basin. She paused after wetting the washcloth to look down at the small splotch of blood on her inner thigh. She slowly wiped the blood away then cleaned between her legs. Her cheeks burned as she felt tender and sore, the evidence of her ruin and the most pleasurable experience of her life.

After washing, she took a purple day dress from her wardrobe and drew it on. Her hands began to shake as she buttoned the back. She had never seen Harry so mad. Before she left her room, she wondered if Robert was all right.

Jackson raised his palm then let it fly. It met Robert's cheek with a resounding crack.

Robert woke with a startle. He looked around lost then blinked up at Jackson through his black eye.

"Morning, governor." Jackson smiled.

Robert looked around him and found he was lying on the foyer floor. "Where is she?"

"Harry dragged her home."

Robert sat up with a groan. His body ached.

"Harry throws a decent punch," Jackson muttered as he inspected Robert's bruised face.

"I know," Robert growled and dragged himself to his feet.

Jackson steadied him with a hand to his shoulder. He let go when Robert nodded.

"How did you know she was here?" Robert asked.

"The whole house knew she was here. Or should I say heard?" Jackson grinned broadly.

"I have to go talk to Harry." Robert sighed.

"You might want to dress first."

Robert looked down to his dirt-and-grass-stained shirt. He grumbled, nodded and then walked upstairs on wobbly legs to change for round two with Harry.

"Robert and I are none of your concern," Alyssum snapped as she stood before Harry in the front parlor.

"None of my concern?" Harry shouted and Alyssum glared. "It is my concern when my best friend deflowers my sister in his office."

"It was my choice. I chose to be with him."

Harry growled and spun on his heel. He took a deep breath before turning back to Alyssum.

"What was your first time like?" Alyssum asked him abruptly, catching him off-guard.

"What?" Harry sputtered.

"Who was she? Did you love her? You didn't marry her, we all know that."

"That's different."

"How?"

Harry sputtered for an answer. "It just is," he finally said. "And what were you thinking, purchasing a dress like that? Where did you get it? Why? Ladies do not wear gowns like that," Harry shouted.

"I'll wear whatever I want," Alyssum yelled back.

"Not while you're in my house."

Robert walked through the front door and entered the foyer. He paused as he saw Violet and Caroline with their ears pressed to the parlor door. Then he heard Harry and Alyssum shouting.

His riding boots clicked on the hard floor and caused Violet and Caroline to turn towards the noise. Violet stared at his bruised face while Caroline stepped away from the door and placed her hands on her hips. Robert took a deep breath and stepped up to her.

"Are you going to let me see her?" he asked.

"Are you going to marry her?"

Robert smiled. "If she'll let me."

Caroline gave a curt, satisfied nod then stepped aside. "You should treat those bruises," she advised before he opened the parlor doors and stepped in.

Alyssum and Harry turned to see who had entered the room. Alyssum's heart jumped at the sight of Robert and his bruises.

"Are you going to let me explain now?" Robert asked as he moved towards them.

"No," Harry replied, then threw his fist.

Alyssum gasped in shock as Harry's fist connected with Robert's jaw. She stepped forward and shoved Harry hard. "Stop hitting him," she screamed.

Robert touched his jaw then flexed it. "That was your last one," he told Harry firmly.

Alyssum exhaled deeply as she found she was exhausted from yelling at Harry. The man was a stubborn as she.

Robert tugged on his coat, straightening it.

"Are you all right?" Alyssum turned and asked him gently.

"I've been worse off." He grinned at her.

"You don't speak to her," Harry snapped and he nudged Alyssum away from Robert.

"I think I just did. Oh look, I'm going to do it again." He turned his body to face her. "You left most of your clothes at my house."

Alyssum eyes widened at his audacity then Robert disappeared from her sight as Harry tackled him to the ground. She threw her hands up in surrender and stepped around them as they scuffled and rolled over the carpet. She was making her way to the door when their voices stopped her.

"You ruined my sister!"

"I love your sister!"

Alyssum turned quickly and looked down to see Harry pinning Robert to the ground by his coats lapels.

"You love her?" Harry scoffed. "You ruin the women you love?"

"I've only ever loved one woman."

"Phft, one huh? Have you forgotten how to count, Robert?"

Robert growled and shoved Harry off him. They both got to their feet quickly.

"You loved Scarlet."

"She is Scarlet," Robert yelled.

"You didn't know that," Harry argued. "Scarlet was a wager you won."

"What?" Alyssum asked quietly.

Both breathing heavily, Harry and Robert turned to her as she spoke.

"He didn't tell you that part?" Harry asked. "That kissing you on the balcony was for money. Oh, and your garter."

Alyssum turned her stunned gazed to Robert. He shook his head at her with a guilty look in his eyes.

"You kissed me for money?" Alyssum asked numbly.

Robert raked a hand through his already messed hair. "I—"

"He made a wager with the men, as he does every year. What did you do last year, Robert?" Harry asked. "Stole a lady's shoe?"

"No one got hurt."

"Well, this time someone did. You got your hundred pounds while Alyssum lost her virtue. Congratulations."

Alyssum turned to leave.

"Alyssum," Robert called out but she had left the room.

She looked to Violet then her mother who stood just outside the door. She hadn't missed the way they had jumped away from the door when she'd opened it.

"Excuse me." She walked passed them and climbed the stairs.

Staring at the closed door, Robert then slowly turned to Harry. They stared silently at each other for a moment then Robert turned and moved to leave the room.

"Just stay away from her, Robert."

Robert swung around and walked back to Harry. "I've been in love with that girl for ten years. Not you nor anyone else is going to stop me now."

Harry eyes narrowed with surprise and shock. "If you've loved her for ten years why haven't you done anything before now?"

"For this exact reason." Robert waved his arms around, indicating to their anger, their bruised faces. "You're like my brother, Harry," he snapped then stormed back to the door. He paused before he opened it, took a deep breath and turned and walked back to Harry.

"Forgot something," he muttered in a harsh voice before letting his arm swing hard. His fist connected solidly with Harry's jaw. Harry grunted under the blow then watched Robert leave the room.

Robert stormed back inside his house, the front door banging shut behind him. He marched back into his office and around his desk.

"Didn't go to well?" Jackson asked as he stood in the doorway.

"No," Robert clipped out.

"Did you see Alyssum?"

"Yes." He remembered seeing the flash of hurt in her eyes as she found out about the wager. He was not losing her. Not over a stupid wager. Not when the wager had helped bring them together.

Robert dug into the bottom drawer and pulled out a black velvet purse. He opened it, pulled a wad of notes out, counted some and then shoved them into the inside pocket of his coat. He placed the rest of the money back in the purse then dropped it back in to the drawer. He walked over to the chaise, picked his coat off the floor, reached inside and pulled out a black garter.

"Going out again?" Jackson asked.

"Yes." Robert placed the garter with the money then walked passed Jackson, into the foyer and out through the front door.

After escaping the confines of her bedroom, Alyssum paced over the lawn at the side of the house. She couldn't handle her mother and Violet's curious, watchful gazes.

Now in the fresh air, she slowly walked back and forth, staring at the grass beneath her walking boots. When she heard the sound of approaching footsteps, she sighed at the intrusion. She wanted to be alone. Turning around, she was about to tell whoever it was to leave her be. She paused when she saw it was Robert. His strides were quick as he walked towards her. She spotted Jackson a few steps behind him.

Robert said nothing when he reached her, but caught her face in his hands and fused their mouth together. She gasped in surprise and held onto his shoulders as he kissed her desperately. Slanting his mouth over hers, he stole her breath, over and over again.

He slowly released her mouth and let his hands slide away, but she pulled him back. Robert sighed into her mouth as she kissed him. His hands came back and cupped her face.

Jackson cleared his throat and Alyssum stopped the kiss and laid her forehead on Robert's. She kept her eyes closed and rested her hands on his chest.

Her eyes opened as he pulled away. Looking up at him, Alyssum raised her hand and touched his bruised cheekbone softly. Her hand dropped as he reached into his coat. She watched with a frown as he pulled out money and a black garter.

Alyssum shook her head, but Robert took her hand and placed the money and her garter in her hand.

"I don't want them if I can't have you," he told her quietly.

Alyssum stared at the money in her hand. "I don't want it." She looked up to him. "I want you."

A smiled spread over Robert's lips.

"What am I suppose to do with it?" she asked.

He shrugged. "Give it Lilly for her help in your ruin."

Alyssum tried to glare disapprovingly but found herself smiling.

"Ah-hem, and what about me?" Violet asked.

Robert and Alyssum turned their gazes and found Violet standing beside Jackson. And beside Violet stood their mother and Harry, and by the looks on their faces, they had been standing there for a while.

Robert watched Harry carefully, waiting for any sudden attacks.

"I was an excellent secret keeper," Violet said.

"So was I," Jackson put in.

"Here." Alyssum offered Violet the money. "Take it."

Violet scooted forward and took the money, but slipped Alyssum the garter back.

"Violet," Harry said disapprovingly.

"It was a gift," Violet replied and looked through the notes. "You can't give back a gift." She smiled up at Harry while shoving the notes inside her skirt pocket.

Robert chuckled then turned his gaze back to Alyssum. Her eyes met his and he squeezed her hand. "I may have kissed Scarlet for a wager, but I fell in love with her because she was you."

Robert's chest expanded as he took a deep breath then asked, "Will you marry me?"

Alyssum gasped in shock while her mother squealed with excitement.

"You want to marry me?" Alyssum asked.

"He better," Harry muttered and their mother smacked his

arm.

"Yes, I want to marry you," Robert answered and shifted his gaze to their audience.

"Why?"

"What?" Robert looked back to her confused.

"Why do you want to marry me?" she spoke quietly.

"I think you heard me in the parlor while Harry was pummeling me."

"You told Harry, not me."

Robert exhaled. "I love you," he whispered to her.

"What was that?" Jackson called out.

Robert glared at him before looking back to a smiling Alyssum. "Happy?"

Alyssum shook her head.

"What now?" he asked. "You want me to get down on my knees and beg?"

"Yes." Alyssum smiled. With a groan, Robert lowered to his knees. He ignored Violet's giggle and looked up to Alyssum from the ground.

"Alyssum Rosewood?"

"Yes?" she asked sweetly.

"Will you marry me and make me the happiest man? Please."

Alyssum tilted head and hummed in thought.

"Say yes," Violet advised.

"Hurry up," Jackson called out.

"You better marry that boy, Alyssum Rosewood," her mother's voice chided her.

Alyssum laughed and nodded. Robert raised his brows in

question.

"Yes, I'll marry you," she answered.

Robert stood. "Harry," he called while smiling at Alyssum.

"What?" Harry grouched.

"You better look away because I'm about to kiss your sister."

Chapter Thirteen

Robert and Alyssum were married two weeks later. Harry had demanded a quick wedding.

They were pronounced man and wife in the town's small chapel. Mr. Potting, the vicar, had performed the ceremony.

Robert had sealed their vows with a strong kiss that had made Alyssum's toes curl inside her white slippers. He had then, to everyone's astonishment, lifted her in his arms and carried her down the aisle and into the carriage.

All the guests traveled to the Lambert estate where the wedding luncheon was being held.

As Alyssum, Violet and Lilly stood to one side chatting happily, the men stood next to each other, watching them.

"Congratulations, Robert. You found your Scarlet and married her," Duke said.

"Well, I'm glad you were able to leave the herd of the ton and join us." Robert raised his flute of champagne to his friend and then took a sip. His gaze traveled over to Alyssum, as it did every few seconds.

"Wouldn't have missed it," Duke replied. "But it seems I missed quite a lot." He noted Robert's bruises.

Jackson laughed. "You missed a whole lot. You should have seen it, Harry and Robert rolling around on the grass. Harry trying to kill him. Robert half-dressed and running for his life."

"Yes, it was all good fun," Robert replied sarcastically.

"Well, it was enjoyable hitting you," Harry said then stopped a passing maid to take a drink off her tray.

"So, one of us is married," Duke sighed.

"And it better stop at that," Tucker said emphatically.

They all laughed at Tucker's seriousness.

"I'm so excited." Caroline beamed then reached over to pinch Alyssum's glowing cheeks. "I'm going to have some grandbabies."

Lilly and Violet laughed.

"It may take some time, Mother," Alyssum whispered and blushed. While Alyssum had been planning her wedding, her mother had been planning the nursery.

"Oh tosh, Robert will take care of that for me."

Violet and Lilly laughed.

"Ah, here are my boys," Caroline exclaimed with a bright smile as Harry, Robert, Jackson, Tucker and Duke stepped into their circle.

Robert moved to stand by Alyssum's side and brushed the back of his hand against hers. Alyssum, uncaring of watchful gazes slipped her hand into his. Robert curled his fingers around her hand with a happy smile.

"Countess, your beauty shines brighter than any star in the sky," Jackson announced as he pressed a gallant kiss on Caroline's gloved knuckles.

Caroline chuckled and beamed

"I would like a dance with my wife," Robert said and looked down to Alyssum.

"But no one is dancing," she replied with a soft smile.

"And?" He arched a brow.

A smile curved Alyssum's lips as she nodded. Lilly took her glass of punch and Robert led her to the centre of the room.

Alyssum hadn't worn gloves for this exact reason. She wanted to feel his hands in hers. Skin to skin. As the violins played and the guests watched, Robert swayed them into a waltz. His hand branded her back as he held her closely and turned her about the room.

Robert lowered his lips to her temple and whispered, "I prefer you in the scarlet gown."

She smiled with a soft laugh and her body relaxed into his hold. Her white wedding gown swished around her legs.

Lilly escaped the watchful eyes of Rickton and her parents. She took solace in these few precious moments when she was alone. But she was only free for a second before someone else entered her haven, the library. She turned from the window and stiffened as she watched Jackson West close the door behind him. Much to her annoyance, her heart skipped a beat then began beating wildly as he stared at her. He approached her, coming closer and closer, making her body come alive in awareness. She frowned at her reaction to him. Her body had never done this before.

"Miss Darrel," he drawled as he came upon her, his height making her tilt her head back. To be more precise, it was her small stature, rather than his height.

"Mr. West," she clipped back, glad her voice was steady.

"So what are we going to do about this?" he asked, slipping his hands inside his pockets.

He shifted closer and she stiffened as his coat brushed

against the bodice of her dress. Her breasts suddenly felt swollen and her nipples ached for touch.

"About what?" she snipped, angered that her body responded to his close proximity. Her gown was now too tight and the room too warm.

"This..." he waved his hand between them, "...heat."

"Heat." Lilly scoffed as her belly fluttered with nerves. "You must be mad."

Jackson grinned. "So you don't want me to kiss you?" he asked, his eyes alight with mischief.

Lilly turned her head to the side, shifting her gaze away from him, from temptation.

Must be a lady.

"I can see it in your eyes," he continued tormenting her. "Your hungry, wanting eyes take me in every chance they get." Jackson leaned closer. "And don't tell me you don't want me. When I walked into this room your eyes practically ripped off my breeches."

That was enough. Lilly whipped her gaze back to him and shoved him, her hands connecting with his chest.

He stumbled back in surprise, a laugh escaping him. "I'm sorry, have I upset you?" he asked in mock sincerity as he stepped towards her, closing the distance between them once again.

"You are no gentleman," she retorted in anger while her body warmed to his closeness.

"No, I'm not." He swooped down and caught her mouth completely off-guard.

Her hands connected with his chest and she shoved him hard. He moved back, releasing her lips.

A gasp of astonishment escaped her as his mouth left hers.

Lilly covered her mouth with her hands as her eyes stared up at him, wide in shock. He had kissed her. Now he just stood there, watching her. Her breath panted wildly against her palms. *Don't. Don't. Don't you dare. Be a lady,* her inner lady screamed to her. But she was lost.

Lilly dropped her hands from her mouth and grabbed his coat lapels. She dragged him forward, stood on her tiptoes and pressed her mouth back to his.

Jackson responded instantly. His caught her face and tilted her head for his kiss. A groan rose from him as he slanted his mouth firmly over hers and took possession.

Lilly held onto his coat and let him sweep her away. Her legs went boneless and her head swirled in pleasure as he kissed her deeply and sinfully. She had never been kissed like this.

He groaned roughly as he thrust his tongue inside her mouth and caressed her. Her back was suddenly pressed into the bookshelf and his body aligned with hers, allowing her to feel every hard inch of him. He stole all sanity from her mind.

Small moans of desire rose from her as he took possession of her entire being with a kiss.

When Jackson suddenly felt Lilly pushing her hands at his chest and not pulling, he released her mouth with reluctance and stepped back. He felt his own breath coming from him in quick, harsh gasps. His pulse was leaping, his blood boiling, his body flaming. He watched her as she regained herself.

Lilly brushed the skirts of her pale blue gown with trembling hands and took deep breaths.

"Ah-hem," she cleared her throat delicately then rose her gaze up to his.

Her expression was cool, the fiery minx now gone, replaced by the prim lady she acted. Jackson missed the minx already.

"Excuse me." She stepped past him and strode across the room. She opened the door then left.

Jackson raised his fingers to his lips. He could still feel and taste her.

He waited a moment before returning back to wedding luncheon. A broad grin curved his lips all the way.

Alyssum looked over the crowd that had joined to celebrate their wedding while she danced with her husband. Her gaze caught and held on something. She furrowed her brows as she watched Lilly appear through a closed door. Her friend's cheeks were flushed and her lips looked...swollen. Alyssum drew her brows closer as Lilly looked around her then walked away. Alyssum gasped as she watched Jackson West come through the same door looking like a satisfied rogue.

Robert followed Alyssum's gaze, having heard her gasp. He saw Jackson and the look on his face. "Hmmm," Robert hummed above her head.

"If he did something..." Alyssum's voice held a strong warning.

Robert twirled her into another direction. "Like what I did to you?" he asked with a wicked grin.

"Exactly," Alyssum exclaimed while trying to find Lilly again.

"Tell me you love me," Robert ordered while smiling down at her.

Lilly and Jackson drifted from her mind as she gazed up at Robert and found him smiling lovingly.

"Why should I?" She smiled.

"I like hearing the truth."

"I like you making me say it."

He lowered his head and caught her mouth with his in a swift, firm kiss.

"Robert," she scolded him. Her mother was watching them.

"Are you ready to talk?" He arched a brow while his eyes held laughter.

She laughed softly and dipped her chin faintly in answer.

Robert grinned. "Say it," he whispered.

"I love you."

Robert sighed deeply in pleasure then leaned down to kiss her lips. This time she didn't scold him but kissed him back.

"Oh and Robert," she whispered as he released her lips.

"Yes?"

"I want a daughter first," she announced with a beaming smile.

Robert's own smile lit up his face.

Much to Robert's joy the guests slowly began to leave. Robert and Alyssum stood by the front door saying their farewells to their friends. As the people filed out slowly, Robert kept one hand on Alyssum's back.

"Be good to him," Jackson spoke to Alyssum.

"I'll try," she replied with a smile.

"Jackson." Robert offered his hand.

"Lambert." Jackson winked to Alyssum then left, walking down the front steps and hopping onto his horse. He was heading back to London.

"Sweetheart," Alyssum's mother cooed and gave her a tight hug. "Now don't be a stranger, you visit anytime."

"I will."

Caroline pulled back with tears in her eyes. She dabbed them with a handkerchief.

"I'm right next door, Mother," Alyssum reassured her. "I'll see you soon"

"But not too soon." Robert grinned. Her mother smacked his shoulder and Alyssum blushed brightly.

Robert's grin slipped as Harry stepped up. They were still on shaky ground.

Alyssum stepped closer to Robert while giving Harry a stern glance that said no hitting.

"You make her cry, even once," Harry said, "I'll shoot you."

Alyssum's eyes widened and Robert nodded with a quirk of his lips.

Harry walked down the front steps and entered the family carriage. Violet waved before the carriage rolled down the drive.

As soon as Robert closed the doors he released a long sigh. "Alone at last," he exclaimed.

Before Alyssum could reply, Robert swept her up into his arms and began carrying her towards the stairs.

"What are you doing?" Alyssum laughed as she wound her arms around his neck.

"Something I've been dying to do for the past two weeks," his impassioned voice rang through the entrance hall as he climbed the staircase.

Alyssum heard the sound of giggling maids and a blush heated her cheeks while desire heated her body. As lust kindled inside her, she leaned in and kissed his ear. A wickedness rose from within her and she took his earlobe between her teeth.

226

Robert half-laughed and half-groaned. She became jostled in his arms and found he was now running down the hall towards the master bedchambers. She laughed at his eagerness and kissed his cheek.

When they entered the bedchamber, Robert kicked the door shut behind him, set Alyssum on her feet and then his mouth was ravishing hers. He took her face into his hands then scattered kisses over her cheeks, jaw and her mouth. Alyssum's light, happy laugh chimed through the room.

With a moan, he set his mouth back to hers and shoved his coat off his body. As the coat dropped to the floor, Alyssum untied his cravat while he unbuttoned his waistcoat. They both discarded the items of clothing then Robert wrenched his shirt from his body.

With his upper body bare, he moved to undress Alyssum.

She felt the tugs at her back as he unlaced her as quickly as possible. She squealed as she heard a tear. "Don't rip it," she cried. "I want to keep it."

Robert kissed her into silence and finished removing her dress, making sure not to rip anymore of the silk. He pulled it down over her body then tugged her out of the material gathered around her feet.

"Married one day and you're already ordering me around," Robert chided while smiling down at her.

Alyssum smiled then laughed as he gathered her back into his arms and took them to the bed. When he placed her on the soft mattress, Alyssum shuffled backwards to the centre and watched as he climbed up after her.

"I have another order," she announced with an impish smile.

Robert grinned then covered her body with his, taking her down onto the mattress. "Do you now?" He tilted his head then

227

leaned in to kiss her neck.

With a moan, Alyssum arched her neck to him and glided her hands over the warm skin of his back. She had missed his touch over the past two weeks.

"Yes," she said, remembering what she wanted to say.

Robert reached down and removed her shoes. He slid his hands under her shift then smoothed them up her legs. He clutched her thighs. "You better tell me now because in a few minutes you won't be able to form any words in that sweet brain of yours."

Alyssum chuckled and pressed a kiss to his cheek. She caught his head in her hands and brought his ear to her lips. "You will be removing your boots this time," she whispered to him then laughed as he groaned. She turned her head and kissed him. As her mouth sent him into a frenzy of passion, he took her hands from his face and wound them around his neck.

"That is an order I can happily see to," he replied against her lips.

With a bright, inviting smile Alyssum, parted her legs.

"Is there anything else you would like from me?" he asked as he removed her stockings, gliding the silk down her legs.

"Yes."

Robert raised his head and looked down at her with a raised brow. "What will it be this time, wife?" he said.

"You have to promise me something."

"What would you like me to promise?" he asked as she wrapped her legs around him.

Alyssum was filled with joy as she stared at the man she loved, her husband, her Robert.

"That you'll never stop loving me," she answered.

Robert pressed his beaming smile against her lips. "Easily

done," he promised. His kiss was filled with all the love and devotion he felt for her. "Easily done."

And just as he promised, in a few minutes Alyssum wasn't able to form any words.

About the Author

At seventeen Tish Westwood read her first romance novel and became an avid reader of the genre. At eighteen she wrote her first novel and by nineteen was offered a contract with Samhain for Scarlet Kisses.

Tish resides in Australia with her family, two cats and two dogs and the wild life in her backyard.

Her heart longs for justice, but her body clamors for sin.

The Runaway Countess
© 2012 Leigh LaValle

Once the darling of high society, Mazie Chetwyn knows firsthand how quickly the rich and powerful turn their backs on the less fortunate. Orphaned, penniless and determined to defy their ruthless whims, she joins forces with a local highwayman who steals from the rich to give to the poor.

Then the pawn broker snitches, and Mazie is captured by the Lord Lieutenant of Nottinghamshire. A man who is far too handsome, far too observant...and surely as corrupt as his father once was.

Sensible, rule-driven Trent Carthwick, twelfth Earl of Radford, is certain the threat of the gallows will prompt the villagers' beloved *Angel of Kindness* to reveal the highwayman's identity. But his bewitching captive volunteers nothing—except a sultry, bewildering kiss.

And so the games begin. Trent feints, Mazie parries. He threatens, she pretends nonchalance. He cajoles, she rebuffs. Thwarted at every turn, Trent probes deep into her one vulnerability—her past. There he finds the leverage he needs and a searing truth that challenges all he believes about right and wrong.

Warning: The delicious, if left-brained, hero might forever change all you think you know about the Robin Hood legend. Contains razor-sharp wordplay, skinny dipping and tortured hearts.

Available now in ebook and print from Samhain Publishing.

It's all about the story...

Romance

HORROR

www.samhainpublishing.com

CPSIA information can be obtained at www.ICGtesting.com
Printed in the USA
BVOW072307100413

317888BV00002B/132/P

9 781619 211384